ONE WEEKEND IN PARIS 1

One weekend in PARIS
USA TODAY BESTSELLING AUTHOR
LISSANNE JONES

One Weekend in Paris

Cover designed by Kim Wilson of KiWi Cover Design Co.

Edited by Karen Hrdlicka at Barren Acres Editing.

Formatting by Lou Stock at LJDesigns

Paperback ISBN: 978-1-922333-18-6

DEDICATION

This book is dedicated to my sweet friend, Kali Anthony, because she loves royal romances as much as I do.

ONE
Nyssa

It was a wintry February Friday evening in Paris, France. Princess Nyssa Dubois of Lecroisa, a small European country located on the Mediterranean Sea, was seated in a small restaurant in the eighth arrondissement, awaiting the arrival of her meal. Her companions for dinner were her American bodyguard, John Ashwood; one of her dearest friends, Arabella von Winthrop, the princess of a neighboring country; and Bella's longtime bodyguard, Dante Rossi.

The two women were next to each other and had talked nonstop from the moment they'd embraced. They didn't get to see each other nearly as often as they might have liked, given Nyssa had been living in the United States in her official role as Ambassador of Lecroisa for the last three years, but they made time for each other. Daily texts, phone or video calls weekly, if they could swing it, and if they happened to be in the same location, they'd meet, even if it was just for a drink and a hug.

They were both in Paris for the weekend to attend an annual charity ball patronized by members of all the European royal families, along with the rich and famous. All money raised was donated to a charity that worked worldwide to free kidnapped women and children who were sold on the black market, a cause both women supported wholeheartedly. Invitations to the ball were highly coveted for those not born into royalty, and the hotel chosen as this year's venue would be packed with people worth billions collectively.

While Nyssa was glad to support such a worthwhile cause, she was even more pleased to be able to catch up with her parents and older brother, as well as her dear friend. While the two women conversed, the men charged with protecting them did the same. John and Dante had met on a number of occasions over the years and got along well.

Nyssa glanced over at the attractive, dark-haired man seated on her right. Her parents had only agreed to allow her to take the ambassadorship if she allowed them to hire a trained security expert to be part of her life in the U.S. John was a former Navy SEAL who now worked in private security, and he was so much more than simply her bodyguard.

He took her to meetings after vetting the people she was to spend time with and the location it was being held at thoroughly. He ensured he was aware of security measures for large events, such as the ball, and all public appearances. He drove her to all work engagements and remained in her line of sight at all times. In the beginning, she'd felt stifled by his constant presence and attention, but John had quickly proven he understood she needed space sometimes and was respectful of that, giving her privacy when she craved it.

But over the last year or so, all she'd craved was him. To be around him. To feel him close to her, breathe in the scent of his aftershave.

Her parents had insisted on buying her a home that came with a sizeable guesthouse out the back, so John was always near her, even when he was off duty. Nyssa had felt it unnecessary he live on her property at first, but six months into her life in the U.S. she'd started receiving letters and packages at her residence.

The packages had spooked her; the initial ones had been full of dead flowers. Next, small dead animals, with notes telling her she was next for rebuffing the unknown sender's advances.

It hadn't taken long for John to locate the man, and once she'd seen the sender's photo she'd realized she'd seen him before. Outside her office. In the café near her office she sometimes liked to patronize because their coffee was good and the muffins delicious. He'd fancied himself in love with Nyssa after seeing her on the local news and had been determined to get her alone, but John had ensured that hadn't happened. The police had been involved, but it had been kept out of the press and the disturbed man had received the medical treatment he quite obviously required.

John had kept her safe.

As time had gone on, Nyssa had realized she enjoyed his company immensely. He was a quietly spoken, intelligent, attractive man who missed nothing. Thoughtful with an excellent sense of humor, he made her laugh like nobody else did.

He made her feel a lot of emotions, some of which she really shouldn't.

And over the course of the last year, she'd come to accept she was in love with her American bodyguard, which both excited and terrified her. They were two people from very different worlds, and there were certain expectations being born into a royal family demanded.

She hadn't even kissed the man properly. There'd been a couple of near misses, when his lips had hovered close to hers while they'd been having dinner at her place. On one occasion their lips had actually touched, only to be interrupted by the sound of his phone ringing. He'd cursed and excused himself, unable to ignore the call, but by the time he'd ended it the moment had been over.

She very much longed to kiss him. To touch him all over. Let him see her bare. Feel his lips explore her naked skin.

Watch him slide deep inside her, giving her pleasure so intense she was sure he'd make her scream.

But for now, she concentrated on what her friend was saying. Arabella was catching her up on the latest gossip and scandal amongst the royal families, as listening to such things was one of Arabella's favorite pastimes.

Their meals arrived, and the four of them continued to talk as they dined. Nyssa ate her fill, then nearly choked when Arabella leaned over to ask something that couldn't be overheard by either of their dinner companions.

"As-tu déjà couché avec lui?" *Have you slept with him yet?*

Nyssa abruptly stood. "Please excuse us, gentlemen. We need to use the restroom." She grabbed Arabella's hand and dragged her to her feet. The other woman grinned broadly and followed her friend over to the women's restroom, which was visible from their table—no doubt why John and Dante had chosen that one in particular.

John got up with them and led the way. He knocked on the door, then stepped inside, allowing it to close behind him. He returned moments later and nodded at them, indicating it was empty and safe for them to enter.

After they'd stepped inside and the door was firmly closed behind them, Nyssa turned on her friend. "Why would you ask me that?"

Arabella raised a perfectly groomed eyebrow. "I just wondered, is all. You've been staring at him all night like you want him to strip you naked and take you right here in the restaurant."

Nyssa let out a horrified gasp. "You lie."

"Do I?"

"Bella, stop it. You know I haven't slept with John."

"Mais tu veux." *But you want to.*

"Vous le savez. Mais je ne peux pas." *You know I do. But I can't.*

"Why not? You're both consenting adults. Neither of you is dating someone else. He wants you just as badly."

Nyssa's heart began to thump loudly in her chest. "You don't know that."

Arabella let out a laugh. "I have two eyes, darling. He's been undressing you with his all night."

The brunette froze in place. "He has?" Her voice was quiet, unsure.

Her redheaded friend reached out to take her hand and squeeze it. "He has. He wants you as much as you want him, Nyssa. What's really stopping you from taking the next step?"

"We're too different."

"You mean because he's not royalty and not Lecroisan? You're worried your parents might not accept him as your chosen partner, and if they don't, then the public may not either." Arabella's astute observation made Nyssa deflate. She accepted a hug from her friend, clinging to her as doubt swept through her. "Nyssa, I want you to listen to me as your dearest friend. Are you listening?"

She nodded. "I'm listening."

"If you truly love him…then fuck what everyone else thinks."

Of all the pearls of wisdom she thought her friend might come out with, that was not one of them. "Bella!"

"It's true. Life is too short not to take a chance on love, especially if you think he could be the one."

Arabella's words gave her much to think about, and she hugged her friend tightly. "Thank you."

"I mean it. Ask yourself this: do you love John? Can you imagine making a life with him? Getting married and having his babies? You don't have to tell me the answer, but don't lie to yourself, darling. And don't lie to him." Arabella gave her hand a squeeze. "I adore John. He's a lovely man and perfect for you."

Nyssa blinked rapidly to stem the sudden flow of tears. "You think so?"

"I know so. Now, let's get back out there to our men before they start to wonder what's going on in here."

They headed toward the door, and then Nyssa realized something, making her stop short. "Wait, what do you mean, 'our men'?"

Arabella turned back around with a broad smile on her face. "Ah, I wondered if you'd heard that."

She studied her friend's face and gasped. "You're sleeping with Dante!"

The redhead looked smug. "Yep. We've been banging for months."

"Why didn't you tell me?"

The smile slid off Arabella's face. "Parce que j'avais peur je te contrariais et je ne voudrais jamais faire cela." *Because I was worried I'd upset you and I'd never want to do that.*

"Oh, Bella." Nyssa's heart ached that her friend had thought she couldn't confide in her. "Why would it upset me? You could have told me. You know I'd be happy for you."

Arabella leaned in and kissed her cheek. "I know, darling, and I adore you for it. But I knew something was brewing between you and John. Besides, I wanted to wait and see if anything serious would come of me and Dante."

Nyssa searched her friend's face. "Do you love him?"

"Not yet." The redhead looked thoughtful. "But I could. Maybe. One day."

They were interrupted by a firm knock at the door. "Is everything okay in there, ladies?"

Arabella rolled her eyes at the sound of John's voice. "Told you! Let's not deprive him of your beautiful face any longer." She flung the door open and gave the man who made Nyssa's heart beat faster a warm smile. "Keep your pants on, Loverboy. We're fine." She patted his chest and breezed past him.

Nyssa was right behind her and she stopped in the doorway of the bathroom to gaze up at a pair of gorgeous blue eyes.

"You okay, Nyssa?"

Impulsively, she got up on her toes and pressed a kiss to the corner of his mouth, something she would not normally have been bold enough to do, especially in public. "I'm fine. I wanted to have a private chat with Bella, that's all."

John's voice was raspy. "Good. It's my job to keep you safe." But they both knew that wasn't why he was standing outside the women's bathroom, and she felt the tug deep in the pit of her stomach. The pull toward him.

He lowered his head until their lips were mere centimeters apart, and then he brushed his against hers. She placed her hands on his hips, waiting for more kisses, but they were suddenly interrupted by a tall blonde woman. "Excusez-moi." *Excuse me.*

Nyssa stepped out of the way. "Bien sûr. Je suis désolé." *Of course. I'm sorry.* She went back to their table, John's hand on the small of her back, and sat after he pulled her chair out for her. Arabella declared they must have dessert before going their separate ways, so the two women looked over the menu. All of a sudden, Nyssa felt a hand slide onto her thigh under the table, and a few moments later she placed her own on top of John's and linked their fingers together.

Dessert was ordered and enjoyed. The four of them chatted about the ball the following evening, and by the time they were done with the meal and the company, the night was black, the wind was freezing, and rain was drizzling from the inky sky.

John paid for the meal with the credit card given to him as part of his employment, leaving a generous tip. He helped Nyssa into her coat before donning his own, as Dante did with Arabella, then the four of them stepped out of the warmth of the restaurant.

Arabella turned to the other woman with a smile. "Do you want a lift back to the hotel, darling?"

Nyssa shook her head at her friend. "Thank you, but it's only a couple of blocks and you're heading the other way. The rain's not too bad. We'll walk."

Arabella raised her eyebrows. "Are you sure? It's no bother. I don't want you catching a cold."

They'd made their way to the restaurant on foot several hours previously, given its proximity to the luxury hotel they were staying at, but it hadn't been raining then.

"I'm sure. We're literally only three blocks from the hotel and will be there in five minutes." She kissed Arabella on each cheek and embraced her tightly as John shook Dante's hand. The American then kissed Arabella, as per European custom, while Dante bid Nyssa goodnight in the same way, and she leaned into John and watched as their companions disappeared into the night.

Once Arabella and Dante were gone, she slipped her hand into her companion's and looked at him. "Shall we?"

His brows furrowed as he glanced up at the sky. "I should have brought an umbrella."

"It's only water, John. We're close to the hotel. If we hurry and stay under the awnings, maybe we'll only get a little wet."

Something in his expression changed, darkened. Nyssa could see it, even in the dim lighting outside the restaurant. Desire and raw hunger swirled in his eyes and her heart skipped a beat as he leaned in so only she could hear him speak. "I think I like the idea of you being very wet."

Desire thrummed through her veins, heating her blood and making her heart race. "Let's go." She took his hand and pulled him out of the doorway. As they stepped into the night from the alcove of the restaurant, they were immediately soaked as the rain got heavier. Nyssa let out a small cry as the fat drops falling from the sky and temperature combined to make her feel as though she was in the Arctic.

John led the way, weaving around Parisians who'd been smart enough to bring umbrellas with them as they ventured out in the dark. They managed to move quickly, despite the rain and people, and were only a block away from the hotel when he suddenly pulled her off the street to stand in the doorway of a boulangerie. The bakery was unsurprisingly closed, given how late it was, but the shop offered cover and a reprieve from the cold spray.

He backed her up against the thick glass of the front display, his body shielding hers. There was no space between them as he took her gloved hands in his and raised them above her head, holding them against the glass. Nyssa felt exposed, despite the fact she was dressed for the cold weather in an ankle-length woolen coat, boots, gloves, and scarf.

"I can't wait another fucking moment."

She opened her mouth to respond, but John didn't give her the chance. Instead, his mouth was on hers and his tongue slid into it, stroking hers in a sensual caress as he kissed the breath from her.

Nyssa heard a loud moan, and it wasn't until he shifted against her that she realized it had come from her. Dear God. She had never been kissed like this before. It wasn't so much a kiss as a possession, and all she could do was give as good as she got.

John released her hands and she immediately wrapped her arms around his neck, holding him close. He broke the kiss, his lips drifting across her face to her jaw. Every touch of his mouth to her skin made her feel warm, her body coming alive under his touch.

When he pulled her closer and rested his forehead on hers, she smiled up at him. "I don't want to stop, but it's really freaking cold out here. Let's go back to the suite where it's warmer, and we can continue there."

He gazed at her intently for a few moments before he spoke. "Nyssa." He spoke her name softly, his breath coming in short pants. "If you don't want this, tell me now and I'll go lock myself in my bedroom." Her suite came with two bedrooms and the second one had been allocated to him, but somehow, she knew he was never going to sleep in that second bed.

She suddenly wished she wasn't wearing so much clothing because she wanted to touch his cheek with her fingers, so instead she brushed her lips against his. "I want this, John. I want you." Another kiss made it very clear she was giving her assent.

He kissed her one last time, a short but fierce kiss, then took her hand in his and pulled her back out into the rainy night. They hurried toward the hotel, and just before they went inside, Nyssa glanced over at the Eiffel Tower, its bright lights visible even through the dark. Paris was one of her favorite places on earth, and now it had become even more special.

Paris would be the place she made love to the man who owned her heart for the first time.

TWO
Nyssa

She blocked out everyone else around her as they walked quickly through the hotel lobby, her only desire to get to their suite and remove her clothing as quickly as possible.

And John's. Damn, she couldn't wait to explore his incredible body, all the muscles and ridges.

The elevator seemed to take forever to arrive, and once it did John swiped the card that would give them access to their secure floor and pressed the button. They didn't speak as they moved upward, but she clung to his hand tightly.

Once the doors opened again on their floor, she followed John to the penthouse suite they were staying in. As soon as the door closed behind her, she was pinned to it by his big, hard body as he kissed the shit out of her, his tongue teasing her and his mouth making her feel hot all over.

He eventually released her and took her hand once more. "Come on, sweetheart. Let's get out of this wet clothing." Once they got to her bedroom, John wasted no time in helping her out of her clothes while also shedding his own. A sense of urgency overtook them both, and it wasn't long before they'd stripped down to their underwear, everything else in haphazard piles on the expensive cream carpet.

She'd had the forethought to wear red lace, and his appreciation was evident, both on his face and by the long, hard length clearly obvious inside his black boxer briefs. Nyssa looked down and gazed at the outline of his cock. Did she dare touch it?

Slowly, she reached out a tentative hand and wrapped it around his dick. When she squeezed gently, the low groan John let out made her smile.

"Fuck, you're beautiful."

She lifted her head to look back up at him, his words making her heart swell and her pussy even wetter than it already was. She was so aroused it wasn't funny, and if she didn't feel this man inside her soon she might just explode.

John moved the straps of her bra down over her shoulders slowly, then reached around to undo it. Nyssa slid it off her arms and let it drop to the ground. Her nipples were already hard and aching for his touch, and when he ran a thumb over one, she couldn't stop the gasp of pleasure that came out of her mouth.

His ocean-blue eyes ran over her body from head to toe, taking every inch of her in. A sudden bout of shyness overwhelmed her, and instinctively her arms moved to cover her bare breasts.

"Don't." His voice was low and rough, as though it pained him to speak. "Don't hide yourself from me, Nyssa. You're fucking gorgeous and I can't believe I'm the lucky bastard who gets to see you like this."

He kissed her softly, slowly, wrapping his arms around her. She could feel his hard cock pressing against her belly, feel his hands cup her ass and squeeze. When he let her mouth go, she pressed her lips against his jaw. "John," she whimpered.

"I know, sweetheart. I'll give you what you need, promise. Go lie on the bed."

She did as she was told, scrambling onto the bed on all fours and flopping onto her back. He climbed onto it with her and began to crawl toward her, his expression predatory. He moved over her, pressing kisses to her rapidly warming skin. After kissing each nipple, the tight buds puckering further, he kissed her lips.

It was a fleeting kiss. He raised himself up and sat back at her feet, his gaze hot and hard as he looked at her. "You won't be needing these." He peeled her soaked panties off, pulling them down her long legs and tossing them onto the floor. His underwear soon joined hers, and Nyssa couldn't help but prop herself up on her elbows so she could look her fill.

His cock was long and hard, jutting straight out from a nest of dark curls in her direction. He was circumcised, unlike most European men, and the head was already glistening with arousal. She wanted to taste him, but before she had the opportunity to do so John coaxed her to lie back and keep her eyes on him before he reached over for a pillow and placed it under her head.

When he spread her legs and settled himself in between them, her heart skipped a beat and the gasp she let loose made him grin. "I'm going to taste this sweet pussy of yours, Nyssa, and then I'm going to fuck you until you scream my name."

Her jaw fell open, and all she could do was nod in agreement. "Okay."

John laughed, and then latched on to her clit without preamble. His hands were around her thighs, keeping her legs spread open wide, and she reached down to clasp his forearms as his tongue worked its magic. Oh, dear God. She could barely breathe as he licked and kissed and swirled and sucked her clit, before running his tongue up and down, up and down.

She whimpered his name and clutched at his arms as she writhed underneath his mouth, gasping for breath. She was ridiculously close to an orgasm already, which had never happened before.

But just as she was about to fall over the edge, he stopped and sat up, wiping his mouth with the back of his hand. “Don’t worry, I’m going to make you come. Can I take you bare?”

She nodded, and he moved until he was on top of her, cradled between her spread thighs. Propped up on one hand, he wrapped the other around his cock and gave it a few pumps before notching the head at her entrance and sliding deep inside her with one smooth stroke.

That was all it took. She came instantly, and he remained balls deep until she stopped trembling around him. “John,” she gasped, her hands on his back.

“That’s my good girl,” he crooned softly. “Look at you, coming all over my cock. You’re so beautiful when you orgasm, Nyssa. I want to see it again and again.”

His mouth came down on hers, and he kissed her as he began to move, thrusting deep into her in long, rhythmic strokes that pressed her into the mattress. All Nyssa could do was hold on to him as he pushed her to another orgasm.

White-hot pleasure speared through her like lightning as she clung to her lover. “So good,” she whispered as her toes curled and her body quaked underneath him.

“So fucking good,” John confirmed. “Your pussy is so tight and wet. You’re going to make me come hard.” Coaxing her up onto her hands and knees, he lightly smacked her ass before pulling her hips back and impaling her on his cock once more. She let out a loud cry as the pleasure became almost too much to bear, his cock feeling too big in this position, stretching her wide open.

"John! You're so big."

"You can take me, sweetheart. You'll give me another orgasm."

"I can't." Nyssa shook her head as he penetrated her deeply, his cock easily sliding in and out of her, the erotic sounds of their skin slapping together ringing in her ears.

"Yes, you can. One more." She felt his lips on her spine as he drove into her relentlessly, his low moans going straight through her. When his thrusts became more erratic, she knew he was close to an orgasm of his own. "Fuck, I'm coming."

She cried out as his cock swelled and pulsed inside her, his orgasm making him moan and hold her close. The feel of him coming inside her body pushed her into another one of her own, and white spots danced in front of her eyes as she almost blacked out.

The front half of her body collapsed onto the bed as she clutched the duvet, her ass still up in the air and her pussy still full of John's cock.

Once they'd both caught their breath, John withdrew from her slowly and she felt the gush of arousal slip from her body. She whimpered, and his lips were on her nape. "Don't move, sweetheart."

"I'm not sure I can," she admitted, and his laugh made her smile.

He climbed off the bed and padded into the large bathroom attached to her bedroom. He returned moments later and she rolled onto her back. He was holding a wet washcloth, and she kept her legs open while he gently wiped her clean.

Once he was done, he threw it far enough for it to land on the tiled bathroom floor and then stretched back out on top of her, propping himself up on his arms so as not to crush her with his weight. She put one hand on his arm and ran the fingers of the other through his hair. His body was covered in a sheen of perspiration just as hers was, and his cock, still impressive even when not hard, lay on top of the glistening dark curls between her thighs.

"Hi." Her tone was soft as she gazed up into the blue eyes she'd grown to love so much over the last three years.

"Hi." He dipped his head and ran his nose along the length of hers. "Are you okay? I didn't hurt you, did I?"

"No, I'm perfect." His mouth crashed down onto hers, and she kissed him for a good long while, enjoying the feel of his naked body on top of her. "Can we do that again?"

He grinned. "I sure hope so. The night is far from over yet." After one more kiss, he rolled over onto his side, taking her with him so they were facing each other. John reached down to grab the blanket neatly folded up at the end of the bed and pulled it up around their cooling bodies.

Nyssa snuggled close, relishing the feel of his strong arms around her. Her fingers played with the dark hair on his chest as he dropped kisses on her face. Did she dare ask the question? Would he answer truthfully? There was only one way to find out, so she took a deep breath and gazed into his eyes. "John?"

"Yes, Nyssa?"

"How long have you known?"

He tucked a lock of hair back behind her ear. "That I'm in love with you?"

She gasped at hearing him say those words out loud. She'd

expected him to admit he had strong feelings for her, but that he'd come out and admitted he was in love with her was a surprise. A pleasant one. All she could do was nod as her heart beat faster.

"About two years."

His response had her rearing back in shock. "Two years?"

The back of his fingers caressed her cheek. "Yeah. I'm guessing it hasn't been that long for you?"

She shook her head, and although she knew it was silly, she felt bad he'd known so much longer than she had. "It's been eight months, three weeks, and four days."

The corners of his mouth curled up. "That's very precise of you, Your Highness."

She slapped a hand over his mouth. "No. Don't call me that while we're in bed."

He kissed the hand covering his mouth and she pulled it away. "Okay, sweetheart." Pressing a kiss to her lips, he spoke once more. "What happened eight months, three weeks, and four days ago?"

"We were at an event and a little girl had a posy of flowers for me. She stepped forward to give them to me and someone in the crowd jostled her, accidentally knocking her over. She started to cry, but you swept her up into your arms and said a few words that dried up her tears and made her smile again."

"I remember her, poor little thing. She was so sweet, wanting to give you some flowers."

"You were so good with her, and when I turned toward you both and saw you holding her, something clicked into place."

His lips met hers in a soft, slow kiss. "Could you imagine me holding our daughter?"

Her eyes widened. How could he possibly have guessed her deepest secret? It scared her a little to admit it, but she couldn't lie. "Yes."

"Good. Because I want to give you a daughter one day. Turn over."

She obeyed, following his instruction and turning away from him as he curled up behind her, his cock hard once more and pressing against her back. He lifted her top leg up and over his own, and she felt his cock sliding between her legs, coating it with her arousal.

Without warning, he pressed into her and glided balls deep. She cried out as his hand covered her breast and rolled her nipple between his fingers, while his lips and tongue were all over her shoulder and neck. "Oh God!" He felt so good inside her, so right. She moved with him as he pulled out of her and pushed back in again and again and again.

Their lovemaking was slower this time but just as good, and she trembled in his arms as she orgasmed, clenching around his cock tightly. He groaned and thrust hard several times before he joined her over the edge, his cock stiffening even more as he climaxed inside her.

Nyssa turned her head toward him and he rewarded her with a long, hot kiss, his hand running over her soft skin before cupping her breast and squeezing it gently.

They lay together like that silently for a few minutes, kissing and touching each other gently. She loved this as much as she did the act of sex itself; the intimacy between them made her heart sing. So when she suddenly felt cold air at her back, she turned over to find her lover standing by the bed, his hand out toward her. "Let's take a shower."

She scrambled up out of bed and took it, walking with him into the large, glamorous bathroom. The large countertop, which contained two sinks, was made of Italian marble. The fixtures were gold, and the tiling on the floor was of the same marble above it. The shower, which ran from one side of the room to the other along the back wall, had two large, square showerheads which jutted out from each side.

John slid open the door to the shower and turned the water on while Nyssa placed a third towel on the heated rack along with the two already there, knowing she'd need it for her hair. Once the water was warm enough, he stepped into the stall and she followed him in, closing the door behind them. He'd turned both showerheads on and it wasn't long before the stall was steamy.

She wrapped her arms around him from behind, pressing a kiss to his nape before resting her head between his shoulder blades. Closing her eyes, she breathed in his scent and his closeness. She was so glad they'd finally confessed how they felt about each other. Perhaps she should have been scared at how fast their relationship was moving; they'd only kissed for the first time earlier that night, and they'd already admitted being in love with each other.

But it felt right. Natural. They'd been heading this direction for years, so now the walls were down she was all in.

"John?"

"Hmm?"

"Je t'aime." *I love you*. Her voice was soft, but she was sure of her feelings. Arabella had been right. Life was short, and love was something she had to grab on to as long as she could.

He turned in her arms and cupped her face, rubbing his nose

against hers before pressing their lips together gently. "Je t'aime aussi avec tout mon cœur." *I love you too with all of my heart.*

She stared at him blankly, blinking rapidly. "Wait a minute. Since when do you speak French?"

He grinned at her. "Since I've been taking lessons with an app on my phone. I wouldn't say I'm fluent, but I can understand some."

"You never told me that!"

"I wanted to surprise you." He dropped a kiss on her nose, then sobered. "You have no idea how hard it's been for me to keep my feelings for you hidden."

She kissed him. "So why didn't you tell me sooner?"

For the first time ever, she saw hesitation and doubt in his expression and she ached to soothe him. "Because I wasn't sure my feelings were reciprocated. Because I'm your bodyguard and you're a real-life princess, Nyssa. It's not as though I can just marry you."

"Says who?"

He cocked an eyebrow. "You think your parents will be okay with you marrying a commoner?"

"I think my parents will be okay with me marrying the man I'm in love with and want to spend the rest of my life with." She kissed him again, biting gently on his bottom lip. "You know I'm not the heir to the throne. My parents aren't going to care that you're not a prince." She hoped they wouldn't, anyway, but she kept any doubt to herself.

Wrapping his arms around her waist, he pulled her close so there was no space between them, their bodies pressed against each other's. "Are you happy?"

"Deliriously so." She threw her arms around his neck as

he dipped her slightly, kissing her long and hard as hot water covered their naked bodies.

Then something else long and hard made its presence known, and she broke the kiss with a smile. "Again?"

"I'm fucking insatiable when it comes to you."

Laughter died in her throat when she saw the intense desire in his eyes. Desire for her. She felt wanted and cherished by the man holding her. "So fuck me hard, John."

"I thought you'd never ask. Turn around and bend over."

He released her and she went to do as instructed, but instead chose to crouch down in front of him so she was eye level with his magnificent cock. The cock that had already given her so much pleasure. It was hard yet again, and when she wrapped her hand around the base it jerked. Holding it steady, she gazed up at her lover then took a long, slow lick from the base to the head before swirling her tongue around and around.

He groaned, his eyes closing and his head falling back. Nyssa gripped his cock tighter and sucked the head into her mouth, sliding it along her tongue. John's hands slid into her hair, gripping her as she hollowed her cheeks and moved her mouth farther down his hard shaft, taking him as deep as she could manage without choking.

She felt powerful, watching as her strong, virile lover moaned while she sucked his dick. She had control, and when she brought a hand up to cup his balls and play with them gently, she felt precum leak onto her tongue. The taste of him was addictive and she wanted more.

She wanted it all.

Suddenly, he opened his eyes and pulled her to her feet. "Bend over." Turning around, she did as he said and leaned on the bench located at the other end of the shower from where they stood.

He pushed her legs open wider and ran the head of his cock up and down her pussy teasingly. “John!”

“Tell me what you need, princess.”

The words poured out of her before she could even think about it. “I need your cock inside me.”

“As you wish.”

He slammed into her without warning and she cried out, taking him so deep she had to get up on her toes. “Oh my God!” He plunged into her relentlessly and all she could do was brace as he fucked her hard and fast. She could feel how wet she was, how big his dick felt inside her, and it was almost too much for her. She moaned with every thrust, his hands holding her hips in place to take him deep.

She came so suddenly she almost fell over, and had John not been holding her she might have done just that. A scream tore from her throat as her body shuddered. He pulled out of her and she felt a gush of arousal flow from her body.

“Holy fuck.” John sounded so pleased with himself that Nyssa couldn’t help looking over her shoulder at him. “You just squirted all over my cock.” She gasped, but before she could say anything he was back inside her, thrusting fast and deep. “I’m going to come deep inside your tight little pussy. Holy shit.”

He did just that moments later, a look of pure bliss crossing his face as his eyes fell closed. His orgasm was intense inside her, and ripples of pleasure washed over her again as her toes curled and her legs shook.

By the time he pulled out, they were both panting for breath. She was still bent over, her hands braced on the wall, unable to move. His lips brushed her spine and then he kissed his way up her body, his hands cupping her boobs and massaging them. “You okay, sweetheart?”

Her body felt unsteady and she decided an honest answer was probably best. “I don’t know.”

“Come sit for a minute.” He helped her turn and sit down on the bench she’d been clutching while he’d fucked her. Hot water continued to flow around them, and when he bent over her she tipped her head up for his kisses until she was able to stand once more.

THREE
John

After they got out of the shower, they dried their bodies and, in Nyssa's case, her hair before stepping out of the large, ornate bathroom.

They didn't bother getting dressed again. He took her hand and led her back to the master bedroom, where they climbed into the large king-size bed together. He got settled with a couple of pillows underneath his head, and then she turned on her side and curled into him. He pulled her close and ran his fingers up and down her spine slowly, gently, and she placed her arm across his chest while throwing one leg in between his.

His dick was dangerously close to her body and he was sure it wouldn't take much for him to become hard again, even though he'd just come three times in less than an hour. The depth of his feelings for the woman lying in his arms surprised John, even though he'd been in love with her for a couple of years.

He'd never truly thought anything sexual would happen between him and the princess he was employed to protect, despite the ever-growing tension and desire that flowed between them. Had he come to believe his feelings were reciprocated? Sure. He'd noticed the occasional flare of lust in her eyes, or the way her gaze raked over his body from time to time. But he'd understood their places in life. She was royalty. He was her bodyguard, the man tasked with keeping her safe in a foreign country.

But now he'd kissed her and seen her naked and been inside her, he couldn't imagine anything different. Where they'd go from here, he wasn't sure, despite her confidence that her parents would be fine with the change in their relationship. If the reigning monarchs of Lecroisa didn't approve of them being together after all, it could mean come Monday, they'd go back to serving the roles they were meant to.

His heart lurched a little at the notion of not being able to make love to Nyssa again after the weekend. If that turned out to be true, then he was damn sure he'd take advantage of their time together in Paris and watch her come as many times as possible.

Her lips brushed against his jaw, and he turned his head to look at her. "You okay, sweetheart?"

She nodded, the corners of her mouth curling up in a smile. "Not sure I'll be able to move for a little while though."

He kissed her lips. "I'm not surprised, given how hard you came in the shower. Didn't expect you to squirt." To his astonishment, a blush crept across her cheeks and she buried her face in the crook of his neck, making him laugh. "You have nothing to be embarrassed about, Nyssa. It was fucking hot watching you come so hard on my cock."

The arm lying across him tightened and he felt her smile against his skin. "That's never happened to me before." Her voice was muffled and she remained hidden, as though shy.

"Good. I like knowing I'm the only man who's ever made you squirt."

"Oh my God, will you stop saying that?"

He laughed even harder and waited until she lifted her head to look at him before placing a hand around the back of it and pulling her down for a long, hot kiss that had her melting against him. His dick stirred and began to harden. "Look what you're doing to me."

She looked down and gave his dick a long, appraising gaze. "I'm liking what I see." Her voice had a sultry tone to it, and it made the body part in question thicken and lengthen even more. She trailed her fingers down his chest and stomach, walking them slowly over his heated skin, until she reached her target and wrapped them around his cock.

He stilled her hand, placing his on top of it. "I need to know something, sweetheart. Is this…." He swallowed, not wanting to say the words but knowing he had to make sure they were on the same page. "Is this just for the weekend?"

Nyssa withdrew her hand and moved into a sitting position, gazing down at him. "I sure hope not. I mean…this is not casual for you, is it?" She nibbled on her bottom lip and pulled the sheet up to cover her breasts.

"Of course it's not." His voice was hoarse, and he hesitated before deciding to tell her the truth. There seemed little point not saying it now. "I'm all in, Nyssa. You know I love you. I want to marry and have babies with you." He reached out, cupped her cheek, and stroked it with his thumb. "If that's what you want, of course. If that's something we can even do."

She released her hold on the sheet, baring her breasts to him once more, and turned her face to kiss his palm. "I want it too."

He pulled her down to him so he could kiss her, and it was quite some time before he let her go. His dick was now completely hard and aching to slide back inside her tight, wet pussy. He leaned in and closed his mouth around one pale pink nipple, feeling it harden underneath the swipes of his tongue.

She let out a loud moan, her fingers grasping his hair, holding her to him. He moved across to the other nipple, laving it with his tongue and tugging it between his teeth.

"John!" Her loud cry had him letting go and lying back down, stretching out on the bed in front of her. He watched as her gaze traveled the length of his body from his face to his feet, then stopped at his hard cock pointing toward the ceiling.

Nyssa moved swiftly and settled herself in between his legs on her stomach, and she gave him a cheeky smile before running her tongue up the length of his dick. "Fuck." When she wrapped her hand around the base and slid the head between her lips, his hips bucked, pushing his dick farther into her mouth. She pulled back, waving a finger at him as though he was a recalcitrant schoolboy, before sucking him back into her mouth and inching her way down until the head of his cock hit the back of her throat.

Her hand moved in time with her lips, stroking the bottom of his cock, and John closed his eyes as he clenched his jaw to stop himself from spilling into her warm, wet mouth. Fuck, she felt so good wrapped around him. "Nyssa."

She stopped what she was doing and let his cock slide out of her mouth with a loud pop. "Yes?"

"Get up and sit on my dick, sweetheart. Right now."

Her excited gasp was followed by her scrambling up onto her knees. She positioned herself over him and took hold of his cock, placing it at her entrance, then slid down in one smooth glide, not stopping until she could go no farther.

They both moaned, and when she clenched around him he pulled her down for a hot kiss. His hands were on her hips, and when she sat back up and began to move up and down he watched, entranced by the way her hips swiveled back and forth and her pussy spread wide open to take his cock deep. She moaned his name and threw her head back as his hand glided up her body to play with her nipples. He ran his thumbs over the hardened tips before squeezing them gently, making her buck against him.

She continued to ride him slowly, taking him deep before sitting up so only the head of his cock was still inside her. He brought one hand down to her clit and toyed with it, which only made her cry out every time she slid down again. It wasn't long before she was clutching his arms tightly, her mouth falling open and her eyes widening as her orgasm hit, making her legs shake as arousal coated his dick in the best way possible.

"That's my naughty girl," he murmured when she slumped over to lie on top of him, his dick still buried deep inside her. "Look at you, coming all over my cock."

"So good," she whispered, lifting her head just far enough to look into his eyes.

He grabbed hold of her ass and held her in place so he could drive his cock up into her hard and fast, and she screamed as another orgasm washed over her. He followed her into the abyss, letting out a long, loud groan as he spilled himself inside her.

Nyssa was still panting when she finally lifted herself up off his softening cock and rolled back onto her side next to him, cuddling up to him. John put his arms around her and kissed her head repeatedly.

"You're going to kill me one day, woman."

Her laugh warmed him all over. "I highly doubt that." She met his lips in a soft kiss. "Are you hungry? I can order some room service." Although it was late, her suite afforded her round-the-clock services, including room service if she wanted it.

"Yeah, I could eat." He reluctantly got out of bed and crossed into the living room to grab the menu, which sat in a folder on a table he knew to be centuries old, while she headed for the bathroom to clean up. Padding back into the bedroom, he found the love of his life propped up in bed waiting for him.

Sliding under the covers, they went over the menu together and chose some meals to share: smoked salmon bagels, omelets, some bacon, and waffles for dessert. John didn't bother getting dressed; the suites they and Nyssa's family were staying in came with a private butler who would simply leave the cart in the entryway for them.

They sat together in bed and talked while they waited for their food to arrive. Fifteen minutes later, there was a knock at the door, followed by it opening and closing again thirty seconds later. As soon as the butler had made his retreat, John got out of bed and wandered buck naked into the entry to retrieve the cart laden with their food. He pushed it into the bedroom and grabbed a couple of spare pillows from the wardrobe for them to use as makeshift tables.

Soon enough, they were propped up in bed and devouring the delicious meal that had been delivered to them. There were some perks to being a bodyguard to royalty; not having to look at prices was one of them. He would never have forked out the amount of money the food cost for himself, but he knew the Lecroisa royal family was incredibly wealthy and money was no object.

But they weren't flashy with it and certainly weren't snobby about it. Far from it. Despite their standing, they were warm, down-to-earth people who treated everyone who crossed their paths with respect, no matter who they were. It was one of the many things John liked about the family.

But he'd seen and heard enough horror stories to know it wasn't just enough for he and his princess to love each other. Even if her parents were fine with their relationship, there was no escaping Nyssa was a princess and politics would come into play. She was not only a member of a royal family, but also heiress to a sizeable fortune. One many men would kill to get their hands on.

Which meant her parents could absolutely veto the idea of a marriage between him and their daughter, and if they did… Nyssa would be left with no choice but to follow their wishes.

And he could lose her forever.

FOUR
Nyssa

The loud, repetitive sound roused Nyssa from her sleep, and it took her a few moments to realize what it was.

Someone was knocking on the door to her suite. Given almost nobody had access to the floor where the royal family was staying, it could only be one of three people: her mother, father, or brother.

"Nyssa? Are you here? Wake up, sleepyhead!"

Her eyes opened fully as she sat up abruptly, suddenly wide awake. Her brother was there, inside her suite, looking for her. If she didn't get up right that moment, he'd likely stroll into her bedroom, expecting to find her alone.

She glanced over at the warm body stretched out next to her, only allowing herself a few seconds to eye her bodyguard turned lover's naked form appreciatively. He had the sheet slung low across his body, only just preserving his modesty against unwelcome gazes. When she finally reached his face, she saw he was also wide awake and ready to spring out of bed at a moment's notice.

"You want me to come out with you?"

She thought for a moment, then leaned over and gave him a soft kiss. "No, it's okay. I'll get rid of Erik. You stay here."

"Nyssa?" Her brother's voice sounded closer.

She shot out of bed and slipped into her silky robe, cinching it at the waist tightly and looking down to ensure nothing was on display her brother shouldn't see. Toeing on her slippers, she opened the bedroom door only far enough to squeeze out of it. "Hi, Erik."

"Good morning." Her older brother was standing in the middle of the large, expensively decorated living room. "I hope I didn't wake you." The curve of his mouth told her he wouldn't be bothered if he had.

Nyssa huffed. "Like you care. What are you doing here this early in the morning?"

His brows furrowed. "Early? It's nearly nine thirty."

Fiddlesticks. She hadn't meant to sleep that long, but John had kept her up half the night, wringing pleasure from her body like she'd never known it. It had been the best night of her life, having sex with the man she was desperately in love with.

But she wasn't sure she was ready to share that with anyone, even her big brother, whom she loved dearly.

"I'm allowed to sleep in, you know. The charity ball isn't until tonight."

Erik grinned. "I know that. I wondered if you wanted to have breakfast with me."

Nyssa raised an eyebrow. "Like you haven't already eaten?"

"Okay, second breakfast, then. Shall we order room service?"

She squirmed in place, trying to figure out how to get her brother to leave without arousing his suspicions. But when she looked at his face, she could see she was already too late.

"Ah." Erik gazed at her inquisitively. "Got a man in your bed, huh?"

"I never said that! It's none of your business."

"So you don't have a man hiding behind the bedroom door?"

"Erik." She glared at him haughtily. "What part of 'none of your business' did you not understand?"

"Who is he? Can I meet him?"

She pointed to the front door. "No, you can't meet him! Out!"

"So there is a man!" Erik stood and straightened up. He looked at the bedroom door, as though he could see through it, then gazed back at his sister. She saw the moment something dawned on him as his expression changed and he tilted his head slightly. "Good morning, John." He spoke out loud, even though there was only the two of them in the living room.

Nyssa gasped and clutched the top of her robe tightly. How on earth had her brother guessed the identity of her lover?

A few awkward seconds passed as she tried to think of what to say next before the bedroom door opened and John stepped out. She looked over her shoulder to see he was fully dressed; he'd put his black pants and white shirt back on, but he was barefoot. He came over to where she stood and wrapped his arms around her waist as she turned back toward her brother. "Good morning, Erik."

Erik gazed at them. "It appears I owe you both an apology for interrupting you."

"No apology necessary. We needed to get up for the day anyway." John placed a kiss on her temple, and she leaned back against him, placing her arms on top of his.

Her brother gave them a soft, genuine smile. "It's about damn time, you two."

Nyssa couldn't hold back her surprise. "What do you mean?"

This made the heir to Lecroisa's throne laugh. "Come on, Nyssa. You think nobody's noticed the way you two look at each other?"

Her eyes widened. "What?" She stepped out of John's embrace and moved closer to her brother. "What are you talking about?"

Erik merely gave her a grin. "It might have taken you both this long to work it out, but it won't surprise anyone else." He leaned over and pressed a kiss to her cheek. "I'm happy for you, little sister. It's obvious you love him."

Nyssa was stunned by her brother's words, but she did give him a quick hug, which he returned. When he released her, Erik looked at John. "What are your intentions toward my sister?"

She smacked her brother's arm. "Leave. Now."

The corners of his mouth curled up, but he ignored her and inched closer to the other man. Nyssa looked at John and his expression was serious, which made her heart sink just a little. She went over to him and laid a gentle hand on his arm. "You don't have to answer him. It's none of his business."

The sound of her voice seemed to pull him out of the trance he was in, and he dipped his head to give her a quick but fierce kiss. "I love Nyssa," he replied, his gorgeous blue eyes gazing at her warm brown ones, even as he answered her brother. "I'm going to put my ring on her finger and my baby in her belly."

Her heart caught in her throat at his declaration. "I love you too," she whispered.

The moment was broken as Erik stepped closer to them and held out his hand. "Welcome to the family, John. I'll say this once: if you hurt my sister or break her heart, remember I'm the future King of Lecroisa and can have you taken out in a heartbeat."

"Erik!" She was appalled at her brother's threat but pleased to see the two men shake hands before Erik pulled him closer in a one-armed hug.

Once the two men separated, John spoke. "Would you like to join us for breakfast, Erik?"

Her brother shook his head and grinned at them both. "It's good of you to offer, but I rather think you two would like to be alone right now. I'll go mooch some breakfast from Maman and Papa instead." He kissed her cheek and headed for the door, throwing a wave over his shoulder as he left.

"Wait, Erik!" Nyssa stepped forward and gazed at her brother. "Please don't say anything to Maman and Papa, not yet."

Erik nodded. "Say anything about what?" He mimed zipping his mouth closed and throwing away a key. "I don't know what you're talking about." Nyssa breathed out slowly, and a sense of relief at her brother's easy acceptance of her new relationship with her bodyguard washed over her.

"Thank you, big brother. I love you."

"I love you too, little sister. It's not my news to share. See you tonight." He winked at her and exited the suite without further ado, and after breathing in and out slowly, she turned back around to her lover.

"That went better than I expected."

John's statement had her turning around and stepping into his arms. She wrapped hers around his waist and held him close. "Yes, it did." She pressed a kiss to his jaw. "Erik would never hurt you."

He laughed and tipped her chin up, his lips pressing against hers in a lingering kiss. "I know he wouldn't. He's just being a protective big brother, and I respect him for it." She kissed him again, then opened her mouth to speak but no sound came out. After a few moments, he kissed her nose. "Tell me."

"Did you mean what you said to Erik?"

"About the ring and the baby?"

She nodded. "Yes. I know it's too soon, but—"

"I meant it. I realize we've only been lovers for a short time, but I know how I feel about you, Nyssa. I'm in love with you. Crazy about you. Have been for two years and it's not going to change. I do want to marry you and get you pregnant." He paused, and she could see uncertainty in his expression. "If that's what you want too."

She beamed up at him. "It is."

He kissed her then, a long, hot kiss that left her tingling all over. Then he abruptly let her go and went over to the phone sitting on the kitchen countertop. "Yes, I'd like to order some room service, please." He rattled off some food and drinks. "Can you please deliver them in one hour? Thank you."

"One hour?"

His gaze swept her body slowly from head to toe and his eyes darkened. Her nipples tightened at the pure lust swirling in them. "We're heading to the shower, where I'm going to spread your legs wide and eat that sweet pussy of yours until you scream. Then I'm going to fuck you until you come all over my cock. I plan to take my time, so one hour."

Nyssa had never had a lover before who spoke the way John did, but she loved his dirty mouth. She was already wet and desperate to feel him inside her. "Lead the way." She held out her hand to him and he took it, weaving their fingers together as he led them to the master bathroom.

FIVE
Nyssa

Nyssa took the hand John held out to her after he'd opened her door and got out of the car. As much as she'd wanted to stroll around Paris, the weather was too cold and the stores she wanted to visit were too far apart, so John was driving the rental car that had been waiting at the airport for them instead.

He'd managed to coax her back into bed after their shower earlier that morning for another round of sex so hot she still felt flushed. Eventually, they'd had a late breakfast, then set out for a couple of hours. They had to be back at the hotel by three to prepare for the ball, but it gave them time to wander around to her usual haunts.

Nyssa had been to Paris enough times to know exactly where everything was. She had two bookstores on her list of stores to visit. The first, which they'd already gone to, was Librarie Delamain, which happened to be the oldest bookstore in Paris. She loved walking the aisles and breathing in the scent of old books; there was nothing like it.

Now, they were approaching the second, better known one—Shakespeare and Company. Located at the end of Rue de la Bûcherie, they had to walk as the road was closed off to traffic and only accessible on foot down a cobblestone path. All stores were on the right, and it didn't take long before they were at the bookstore and its attached café, which sat at the end of the road.

The café had wooden seating outside, located underneath cream awnings and umbrellas. A few hearty souls were enjoying some baked treats and hot drinks outside, but hopefully there'd be a couple of spare seats inside the café once they were done shopping.

She stepped inside the bookstore, her hand still firmly entwined in John's, and smiled. There were books as far as the eye could see and she couldn't wait to explore the bookshelves stuffed to the brim.

"Take your coat off, sweetheart." She stuffed her gloves inside one pocket and allowed him to help her remove her coat, then held on to it while he did the same with his. When he took hers and folded it over his left arm on top of his own coat, she bestowed a soft kiss on his lips in thanks. It meant she could wander freely and look at all the books clamoring for her attention.

The rare book section called to her first, and John stayed close behind her, browsing a shelf or two himself. Nyssa spotted a couple of books she was interested in but decided to think on before purchasing. She went from section to section, showing her man a book here and there.

By the time she was done, she had an armful of books to take to the register. After purchasing a branded tote to carry them all in, she allowed John to take the bag off her as they made their way next door to the café. They managed to find an empty table, and after perusing the menu, Nyssa made her selections while John went to the counter to place their order.

He kissed her as he sat down next to her, and she shuffled a little closer to him. The café's menu was not extensive, but there was a good enough selection to choose from. They decided to share a few desserts, so settled on a slice of lemon pie, a chocolate muffin, and scones with butter and jam, along with coffee for both.

She fed him pieces of their desserts in between kisses, and there was nowhere else in the world she would rather have been at that moment—and with nobody else. Sliding an arm around his neck, she kissed him longer than polite company would have deemed necessary, but they were tucked away in a corner and nobody was looking at them.

Once they were done, they put their coats and gloves on and headed back to the hotel. They had about half an hour before they needed to commence getting ready for the ball, so they spent that time lying on the bed in each other's embrace, talking and kissing.

Eventually, it was time for them to begin preparation for the evening's activity. Nyssa had declined her mother's invitation to get ready with her parents and use the queen's attendants to help her prepare. She'd been doing her own hair and makeup since she'd moved to the U.S. and was perfectly capable of making herself up appropriately. She even preferred to do so these days.

They took a quick shower together to freshen up, then John disappeared into the bedroom he'd originally been allocated to dress in his tuxedo. Nyssa took advantage of the time alone to slip into the new lingerie she'd brought with her in the hope perhaps her bodyguard would see what it looked like on her. Thankfully, now that their physical relationship had begun, she'd do just that before the night was over.

By the time John came back into the master bedroom, she'd already donned her gown. Made of a deep red silk, it was long sleeved with a high neckline, as protocol dictated. She wasn't allowed to show off any of her assets while at events where she represented her country. It tucked in at her waist, then flared out, the hem near her ankles. Her high heels were the same color, and she'd decided to forgo wearing a necklace in favor of drop ruby and diamond earrings which matched her tiara.

She was still bare faced, her tresses hanging loosely around her head. Normally, she'd have done her hair and makeup first before donning her dress, but since she had to put it on over her head she didn't want to risk ruining her hair or getting makeup on the gown. Since she was dressing alone, it was easier for her to put her gown on first. She watched as John's gaze slowly traveled the length of her body and back again. "You're so fucking beautiful you take my breath away."

Nyssa smiled and held out a hand to him. He took it and brought it up to his lips so he could kiss the back of it. "You scrub up quite nicely yourself, Mr. Ashwood." Stepping forward, she adjusted his slightly crooked bow tie and brushed lint off his shoulders. "Every woman in the ballroom will be drooling once they get a look at you."

He gave her a toothy grin. "Too bad for them my heart has already been stolen." He pulled her into his arms and kissed her, deep and slow.

"I'm never going to give it back, you know." Her voice was soft and breathy.

"I don't want it back, Nyssa. It's yours. Has been for years." After one more kiss, he let her go so she could finish getting ready.

Half an hour later, her face was perfectly made up and her hair swept up off it in an elaborate style held in place by her favorite tiara. The diamond and ruby headpiece had been a sixteenth birthday gift from her paternal grandmother, who'd then been queen, and she loved it.

Once she checked she had her essentials for the evening, she made sure John's pockets held everything safely. She'd taken up her lover's offer to save her having to tote around a clutch all night, and not for the first time she lamented the lack of decently sized pockets in women's clothing.

Since they were going straight from their hotel room to the car to the venue, she opted not to bother with a coat. The large ballroom would be heated, so it was unlikely many of the guests would choose to wear heavy coats that would simply get in the way. Once they were ready, they went down into the hotel's private garage and got into their car. John put the heating on, and soon enough Nyssa was warm enough to forget it was an incredibly cold winter's evening in Paris.

She stared in wonder at the lights which blazed around the city as they drove the five minutes from the eighth arrondissement, where their hotel was located, to the sixteenth arrondissement, where the event was being held. She found herself wishing the drive had been a little longer, just so she could stare at the lights and the stars twinkling above them in the inky black sky.

They arrived at the venue for the evening and left their car with a valet after John helped her alight from the vehicle. Hurrying inside, they entered the elaborately decorated ballroom and looked around. Nyssa studied the room in wonder, even though she'd been to hundreds of similar events over the course of her life. There were flowers as far as the eye could see; large arrangements dotted the perimeter of the room, while smaller ones sat in expensive crystal vases on the tables.

There were ten people allocated to each one, and each place

held china gilded in gold with solid gold cutlery. Heavy crystal glasses sat at the head of each setting, with linen napkins artfully folded on the top plate.

Wait staff circled the room carrying trays filled with champagne, beer, soda, and water. Others had bite-sized canapés. Nyssa snagged two glasses of champagne while John grabbed some canapés, and once she spotted her parents they made their way through the crowd to reach them.

"Bonne soirée, Maman, Papa." Placing the glasses down on the table, she kissed both her parents on the cheek in greeting.

"Good evening, Your Majesties." John bowed deeply, and Nyssa's heart warmed at his sign of respect.

Queen Manon held her hands out to the American and he took them, then placed a kiss on each cheek before shaking the king's hand. "Good evening, darlings," she greeted them both warmly. "You look wonderful. Nyssa, that dress is gorgeous on you."

While Nyssa usually spoke in French with her parents, she loved that they stuck to English in John's presence, aware he would not be able to follow their conversation otherwise.

"You look so beautiful, Maman." The queen wore a dark blue gown which suited both her figure and stature in life nicely, and her hair and makeup were flawless. The diamond crown she wore was heavy, Nyssa knew from the one time she'd borrowed it, but her mother wore it effortlessly.

"She does, doesn't she?" This came from Nyssa's father, who nodded toward his daughter. "Like mother, like daughter."

The four of them sat at the table and chatted for a little while; they'd had lunch on Friday after Nyssa and John's arrival in the French capital, so the conversation was appropriately light for the location. Erik soon joined the quartet, and not ten minutes later Arabella and Dante arrived to greet Nyssa's family. Her parents and sister would make up the ten people needed for the table, and Nyssa was glad she knew everyone she was sitting with.

After a little while, her parents left the table to mingle with other royal guests, leaving the children and their partners alone. The three men conversed about sports while the two women gossiped about the other guests at the ball.

Eventually, everyone was seated as dinner was served, then once the elaborate, seven-course meal had been digested people drifted off to dance, talk, and participate in the various silent auctions situated around the room. Nyssa watched her parents wander around, talking to other monarchs, before accepting John's offer to take a walk around the room with him. As much as she might've liked to, she couldn't spend the entire evening in her seat. They strolled around the room, stopping to chat with other royals as they went.

Sometime later, she smoothed down the silk of her ankle-length dress as she sat back at the table she'd been assigned to. Reaching up, she touched the tiara which sat in a perfect position on her head, her hair artfully styled around it in a chignon which highlighted her delicate features, to ensure it was still pinned in place.

Erik was on the edge of the dance floor, deep in conversation with John. She was curious to know what her brother and lover were talking about, but not enough to go over and interrupt them. She wanted to catch her breath for a few moments and have a drink.

The two chairs on either side of her were empty. Erik had

been seated on her left, John on the right. Bodyguards were usually seated at a separate table nearby, but for this ball she'd listed him as her date, so he'd been seated next to her.

She liked it. She liked having him close to her.

Nyssa had attended so many of these events she'd lost count. Engagements, weddings, anniversaries, christenings. The occasional funeral, obviously more somber affairs. While she always enjoyed seeing her family, especially since her move to the U.S., and loved catching up with friends like Arabella, she'd grown tired of having to dress up in thousands of dollars' worth of clothing and jewelry. Tired of having to make small talk with people whose company she didn't particularly enjoy, such as the prince who always spoke to her breasts, rather than her.

But this ball was for charity, and helping raise money for worthy causes was always something she'd make time for.

She looked over at John, and as though he somehow knew where her gaze was, he turned his head to look at her. When he winked, the corners of her mouth turned up.

"There you are!" Arabella plopped into the empty seat next to her, a champagne flute in each hand. Nyssa accepted the heavy crystal glass with thanks and sipped the cold, expensive liquid inside it.

"Here I am. Are you having a good time?"

Arabella threw back a mouthful of her drink before answering. "Eh. Ran into Prince Caspian a little while back. He's still a frightful bore." She imitated being asleep by lolling her head to the side and pretending to snore, which made Nyssa laugh.

"You're terrible."

"But truthful." Arabella was dressed in a gorgeous green

gown, the shade matching the color of her eyes and jewels. "Can we leave yet?"

Nyssa let out another laugh, bringing her glass back up to her mouth for a drink. "Not yet, darling." She couldn't stop herself from looking over at John and smiling.

"Oh my God!"

Arabella's exclamation had Nyssa whipping her head back to look at her friend. "What's wrong, Bella?"

The redhead's eyes were wide. "You had sex with John."

The statement made Nyssa choke, and she started to cough violently. Out of the corner of her eye she saw movement, and realized John had seen her drink go down the wrong way and was starting toward her. She held up a hand and he stopped in place.

Arabella patted her back helpfully. "You okay?"

Nyssa coughed a few more times, then picked up the glass of water in front of her and took a long drink. When she'd calmed, she looked at the woman sitting next to her. "If you're trying to kill me, I wouldn't suggest doing so in such a public setting."

The other princess threw back her head and laughed. "Why would I try to kill you, darling? Who else would I gossip with at these events?" She leaned over and pressed a kiss to Nyssa's cheek. "Stop deflecting. Tell me. You banged John last night, didn't you?"

Nyssa's gaze went straight back to John, and she could see the concern on his face. She gave him a bright smile to let him know she was okay, and he relaxed a little before turning back to her brother, who just seemed amused.

"What sort of question is that to be asking in public?"

"Would you rather we go somewhere private to talk?"

Nyssa looked around. There were very few people at the tables at this time; most were either dancing or standing around in groups conversing. "No, it's okay. There's nobody within earshot."

Arabella raised her perfectly shaped eyebrows. "Don't want to venture far from your lover?"

Nyssa narrowed her eyes at her friend. "What makes you think he's my lover?"

The other woman snorted. "Are you joking right now? You two have been eye fucking each other all night."

Her mouth fell open. "Arabella! I can't believe you just said that."

Arabella grinned at her. "You're still not denying it."

Nyssa let out a long breath and sighed. "If I did deny it, then I'd be lying." The shriek her friend let out was loud enough to turn a few well-coiffed heads, and she placed a hand on Arabella's arm and squeezed it. "Bella, for heaven's sake! Stop drawing attention to us, will you?"

Arabella slapped a hand over her mouth until she quieted. "I'm sorry, darling. But this is so exciting! I need all the details. How did it happen? Did you run back to the hotel last night and jump him straightaway? How big is his dick?"

Nyssa closed her eyes briefly. She loved her friend, but the other woman had no filter sometimes. "I need another drink."

Arabella caught the eye of one of the countless waitstaff strolling around the room with laden trays and snagged two more glasses of champagne with thanks. She waited only long enough for the waiter to be out of earshot again before she spoke. "I'm waiting."

After Nyssa had drained half the glass, she took a deep

breath and looked at her friend, who was practically bouncing in her seat like an excited puppy. "Okay, fine. In order: he kissed me on the way back to the hotel last night up against the window of a boulangerie, we definitely jumped each other straightaway, and big enough to be satisfying."

Arabella clapped her hands together excitedly. "That's fantastic! How many times did you do it?" She paused to look around and make sure nobody was eavesdropping on them.

"Three or four times before we got some sleep." Arabella's eyes danced with delight as the brunette continued, "By the time we got back to the suite, we…" She trailed off as a blush stole over her cheeks and uncharacteristic shyness washed over her. "Well, our clothes were wet, you see."

"So of course, you had to take them all off." The sly look her friend gave her made Nyssa laugh.

"Of course. Couldn't risk catching a cold."

Arabella's expression softened as she reached out to take Nyssa's hand in her own. "Do you truly love him, darling?"

She breathed in and out before nodding. "Yes, I do."

"And he loves you?"

"He does."

"Then good. I'm happy for you both. Does your family know yet?"

"Erik does." Nyssa groaned as she thought about that morning. "He came to my suite this morning to have breakfast with me, and we were still asleep."

"He caught you in bed with your bodyguard?"

"Oh my gosh, no. We were dressed." She paused. "Sort of."

Arabella's peal of laughter made her smile. "How did he take it?"

"Good, actually. He didn't seem surprised at all."

"See? I told you. Eye fucking."

"Arabella!" Nyssa reached for her champagne and downed it all in one gulp, hoping her mother wasn't watching her at that very moment. As a princess, it had been ingrained in her to be aware of what she said and did in public at all times.

The other princess rubbed her hands together. "Now, let's get to the good parts. How big is his dick, did you say?"

Nyssa had to fight to stop a huge smile spreading across her face. "I didn't."

"It must be big. There's no way it can't be! He exudes big dick energy, always has."

"Let's just say, the energy is not wrong and leave it at that."

Arabella threw back the rest of her champagne and pouted. "Fine. How many orgasms did he give you?"

Nyssa stopped to think. "Uh…"

The redhead's eyes widened. "So many you lost count?"

She leaned forward, even though nobody was around them, so they absolutely could not be overheard. "We had sex half the night, Bella. In the bed, in the shower, against the wall. And in the shower, something happened to me that never has before."

Arabella looked deep in thought. "Like what?"

A blush heated Nyssa's face and she was sure it was so red she resembled a tomato at that moment. "He made me come so hard I—" She couldn't bring herself to say the word. Although the topic of their conversation was hardly appropriate for the gathering they were at, Nyssa was glad she had her close friend to talk to about such things.

Arabella stared at her for a few moments, then her eyes widened and her mouth fell open. "Oh my God! He made you squirt?" She lowered her voice to a whisper, but it still sounded loud.

Nyssa patted her hot cheeks. "Yes."

Arabella snagged two fresh glasses of champagne from a passing waitress and handed one to her friend. "That deserves a toast, don't you think?" They clinked their glasses together. "To bodyguards with big dicks who make you come so hard you squirt."

Nyssa hid her laugh behind a cough but couldn't stop it when Arabella gazed around the room and, after catching John's attention, raised her glass to him with a big grin.

"Bella!"

"What? Sounds like the man deserves a toast, at least. Or a really good blow job."

Nyssa choked, glad the glass she was holding hadn't yet touched her lips. "You're incorrigible."

"You love me." She drained her glass then stood, holding a hand out to Nyssa. "Shall we go dance, or are you too sore for that after your night of marathon sex?"

Nyssa stood, downed a mouthful of champagne for courage, and took her friend's hand. "Please don't say anything."

"Of course not, darling. You know you can trust me."

The two princesses hit the dance floor. Arabella immediately got into the groove with the upbeat, fast-paced song only younger attendees were dancing to, and soon enough Nyssa joined her friend, swaying her body in time to the music.

"Mind if we join you?" Nyssa turned around to find her brother and lover standing right behind her.

"Of course not, Erik. Come dance with me." Arabella held out a hand toward Nyssa's brother, and he dropped a kiss on it before taking it.

Nyssa smiled. Erik and Arabella had always had a flirty type of friendship, but she knew neither was attracted to the other romantically. They were simply both people who'd been born into royalty and understood, as very few did, what it was like to live such a lifestyle. Arabella was the crown princess of her country, as Erik was the crown prince of theirs, and one day she'd be queen, just as he would be king.

"I guess that means you get to dance with me." John's familiar, deep voice was close to her ear, and Nyssa shivered as she stepped into his arms.

"It's a tough job, but somebody's got to do it." The smile she gave him belied her words, and just as she took his hand the song ended. The one that followed was better suited to slow dancing, which suited Nyssa just fine.

They swayed together, not speaking. John wrapped an arm around her waist, holding her more closely than was appropriate as her bodyguard, but was just fine as her lover. His free hand held hers, and she placed her arm around his neck, her head on his shoulder. She could feel his heart beating, and the sound made her own heart swell. The love she felt for the man holding her was immeasurable.

"Dare I ask what you and Arabella were discussing at the table?"

She straightened up and laughed. "I don't think you want to know."

He grinned at her. "You're probably right, but I am curious as to why she raised her champagne at me."

"Oh God." Her face flushed, and it made John's grin get even wider.

"Tell me, sweetheart."

"I…" She paused for a few moments. "I told her about what you did to me in the shower last night."

He raised an eyebrow and leaned in so his mouth was right next to her ear. "You told her I made you squirt all over my cock?"

She avoided his gaze. "Yes."

His laugh made her relax. "I'm glad you have a friend to talk to. I like Arabella."

Stepping closer to him, she left no space between them. "So do I. She won't tell a soul."

"I'm not worried, Nyssa. You can tell her whatever you like. Did you also tell her how much I love you?"

This had her tipping her head back far enough to gaze into his beautiful blue eyes, eyes she could get lost in. "Yes." She wanted to kiss him so badly, but it was important to her that she tell her parents about the change in their relationship before the entire world found out, so she kept her lips to herself.

But it was harder than she imagined not to press them against the man who held her in his embrace. And suddenly, her parents' blessing felt critical.

Or her relationship with her bodyguard might not last longer than one weekend in Paris.

SIX
Nyssa

Nyssa knew she was standing far too close to John, but despite the fact they were dancing in a room full of people, she couldn't bring herself to put even an inch of distance between them. Being in his arms was the only place she wanted to be that night, and for the first time in her life she resented having to perform royal duties and attend this ball instead of being back in her hotel suite, naked and taking pleasure from her lover's touch.

She was fiercely aware of his hand on the small of her back and her fingers wrapped around his. Her lips were entirely too close to his as they gazed at each other, moving in time to the music. She glanced around and was dismayed to see more than one pair of eyes trained on them. "People are watching us," she whispered nervously.

"Of course they are." His voice was as low as hers. "I'm dancing with the most beautiful woman in the room."

Nyssa couldn't help but beam at him as a blush pinked her cheeks. "You've already seen me naked. You don't have to flatter me now."

"I'm just stating the truth." He dipped her as the song ended. "Want to go somewhere private and make out for a bit?"

Her laugh had him grinning back at her. "Yes." She gave him a mischievous look as he released her and led the way out of the ballroom. They took cover on a balcony, away from prying eyes, and Nyssa shivered from the bone-chilling cold.

John opened his arms and she stepped into his embrace, warming as he wrapped his jacket around her as well. She tipped her head back and was rewarded with the feel of his lips on hers, and it wasn't long before the cold had been banished as his tongue stroked hers in a long, hot kiss.

When they finally broke apart, he rested his forehead on hers as they both sucked in lungfuls of cold air. "I think I like this better than dancing in a room full of people, even if it's colder than the Arctic out here."

"I like this better too." She gave him another passionate kiss. "But I think we ought to get back inside before someone notices we're missing." Nyssa knew Arabella or her mother would realize sooner rather than later that they were not in the ballroom with all the other attendees.

John took her hand in his but dropped it just as they reached the ballroom doors. He stepped aside to allow her to enter ahead of him but stayed close behind her.

"There you are!"

Nyssa suppressed a groan as a tall, blond man suddenly stepped into view. As much as she would have liked to excuse herself from his presence, manners wouldn't allow her to do so. "Good evening, Arthur."

Arthur was the crown prince of the tiny country which sat to the west of her own. Living in Washington D.C. meant their paths didn't cross all that much, thankfully. Arthur's family and her own were friendly and had spent time together over the years, and of course they all attended the same functions and events around Europe. It wasn't as though she disliked him, but more that they were very different people and didn't have much in common.

She felt John's hand on her back, rubbing it gently, and it helped her relax as Arthur took her hand in his and brought it up to his mouth, pressing a kiss to her fingers. "Nyssa, darling. Enchanting as always."

She gave him the smallest of smiles. "You're too kind."

"I've been looking for you all night! I humbly request a dance."

"I would, Arthur, but I really must—"

"I insist." The corners of his mouth curled up, but the smile he gave her didn't make her want to return it.

She hesitated for a few moments, then placed her hand in the one he held out to her. "Just one. I can't let you be greedy and keep me occupied all night!" She tried to keep her tone light and teasing, and the broad smile the prince gave her told her she'd succeeded.

She glanced over her shoulder at John, and she couldn't miss the way a muscle in his jaw ticked as she stepped away from him. His body was tense, his expression blank. Nyssa knew he didn't like Arthur touching her any more than she did.

"It's okay," she mouthed at him. "I love you."

His eyes softened, but he followed them and she was grateful for his closeness.

Arthur spun her into his arms, standing uncomfortably close. Nyssa pulled back far enough to put a polite distance between them as they twirled to the music. She spotted John talking with Arabella, and then her friend looked over to where Nyssa danced with Arthur. Arabella frowned as John whispered something in her ear, and then she stepped onto the dance floor with him, her hand in his.

"Staring at your bodyguard?"

Arthur's question interrupted her train of thought. "No. I was trying to find Arabella, but it seems John has located her for me." As hard as it was, she focused on the man she was dancing with, asking after his family and his work. She knew he was based in London and his work involved stocks or shares or something along that line, but she didn't know the details and didn't really care to.

"How old are you now, Nyssa?"

His question threw her. "Twenty-nine."

He appeared to be thinking her answer over. "So you'll be thirty in October?"

"Yes." She wasn't sure whether to be concerned he remembered her birth month or not. "Why do you ask?"

He gave her a wide grin. "Just thinking ahead. How about a Christmas wedding?"

The song stopped, and couples separated as they clapped politely. But Nyssa tuned everyone out as she stared at the man in front of her. Pulling her hand out of his and putting some space between them, her brows furrowed. "What on earth are you talking about?"

"I thought you'd like the idea of a Christmas wedding, but I suppose we can wait until next year to marry. I would rather do it sooner than later though, because I plan to get you pregnant as soon as possible."

Her eyes widened so much she was surprised they didn't fall out of her head. "Are you well, Arthur?"

"Of course I am. Why wouldn't I be? I can't wait to marry you."

"Marry me?" She took a step back and gazed at him in dismay. "There's never going to be a marriage between us. Are you insane?"

Arthur frowned, then cocked his head and gazed at her. "You don't know, do you?"

Nyssa balled her hands into fists at her side. "Know what?"

"That we were betrothed by our fathers as children. If neither of us were married by the time we both reached the age of thirty, then we would marry and join our royal families together."

Acid burned her throat as she struggled not to throw up. "I—" She was horrified to find herself suddenly blinking back tears.

Arthur's brows furrowed as realization dawned. "You really don't know what I'm talking about, do you?"

Nyssa shook her head. "No, I really don't."

"Come with me and I'll explain somewhere privately." He held out a hand to her, and after a few moments of hesitation she took it. Despite his somewhat stuffy public persona, she'd known him long enough to know he had a good heart and wouldn't lie to her about something so important.

He led her through the ballroom full of guests, stopping to exchange a few words of greeting when necessary. Nyssa looked around and saw John was following them, which made her breathe a sigh of relief.

Finally, they made it out of the room. Arthur stopped in the long hallway outside, looking both ways. Guests obviously attending the ball judging by their attire milled around, perhaps needing to catch their breath or get out of the crowd.

"Over here." Arthur pushed open a small door out of the way of prying eyes and flicked on the light. It appeared to be a small storage room; tables were stacked two high against the three surrounding walls, with rows of chairs in between. There was more than enough room for them to stand and talk, however.

John followed them both into the room, and then a few moments later the door opened once more to reveal Erik hot on their heels. The two men moved to flank Nyssa on either side, and she was grateful for their calming presence because she was nervous about the conversation she was about to have.

Arthur glowered at both men. “Do you mind? This is a private conversation between me and Nyssa.”

Erik merely raised an eyebrow. “Anything you have to say to my sister you can say in front of me, Arthur.”

The other man sighed, then looked over at John. “I don’t suppose you’re leaving, either?”

Nyssa felt her lover’s hand on the small of her back. “No.”

“Fine!” Arthur’s exasperation was evident. “Let’s just get this over with. Nyssa, our parents came to an agreement when we were younger to state that if neither of us were married by the age of thirty, we would marry each other to strengthen the ties between our two countries.”

She couldn’t stop the gasp escaping her lips, and when she looked at her brother, his expression told her he was just as surprised as she was. There was no way Erik knew anything about such an agreement because he would never have kept it secret from her.

It wasn’t possible. Her parents would not have agreed to such a thing because they would never force her to marry a man she didn’t love. It simply had to be a mistake on Arthur’s part. She narrowed her eyes and gazed at the blond man standing in front of her. He looked a little peaked, his cheeks red and his eyes glassy.

"Arthur." She put her hands on her hips. "Have you been drinking schnapps again?"

The loud snort of laughter came from her left, her brother making no attempt to hide his amusement. When she glanced right, she noticed the corners of John's mouth twitching, but he was much better at containing his reaction to her question.

All the occupants of the room knew why she was asking. Over a decade ago, when she and Arthur had both still been teenagers, his family had been visiting hers one summer. Arthur had been introduced to schnapps by her father and had indulged a little too much in his new favorite tipple. Both families had discovered him swimming in the large fountain smack bang in the middle of the gardens, and since the evening had been quite warm, he'd removed all his clothing before doing so.

Her parents had been incredibly amused by Arthur's drunken exploits, but his, not so much. She'd told John about the evening after the first time he'd met Arthur, because the prince had been a pompous prig to her bodyguard.

Arthur's gaze became steely as he stared at Nyssa. "No, I have not been drinking schnapps!" he hissed. "And I'm not making this up, Nyssa. You know me better than that."

Her face softened. She did know that. Arthur may have been a lot of things, but a liar he was not. "I know you're not." She kept her tone warm, trying to soothe him, because she was beginning to suspect something was very wrong. "I'll speak with my parents about it."

Following her hunch, she reached out and took his hand in hers. "What's really going on here, Arthur? You know you can tell us if something's bothering you."

His face suddenly distorted as though he was in pain, and suddenly the mood in the room changed rapidly. Any trace of laughter disappeared from Erik's expression, and even John looked concerned. Arthur squeezed her hand, and her heart began to ache. Something was terribly wrong, and her irritation at his earlier behavior was instantly forgotten in the face of his distress. "Oh, darling. Tell us what's wrong. Perhaps we can help."

Erik placed a hand on the other prince's arm. "Nyssa's right, Arthur. If we can help, we will."

Arthur's shoulders sagged, as though he were literally carrying the weight of the world on them and it'd suddenly become too heavy for him to manage, and his chin dropped so he was staring at the floor. "You can't help. There's nothing anyone can do."

"Do about what?" Nyssa squeezed his hand in support.

They gave him a few moments to compose himself, and he opened his mouth as if to speak but then closed it again, shaking his head.

"Would you like me to step out of the room, Your Highness, so you may speak freely?" John's question to Arthur made her heart swell. That he was offering to leave and referring to Arthur by his title was a show of respect, and she loved him all the more for it.

Arthur sized John up for a few moments, his gaze blank. Then he let out a long, almost painful sigh. "No, it's okay, John. I appreciate your offer but since I'm quite sure Nyssa will only confide in you later, you may as well stay." Taking a deep breath, he pivoted slightly toward the two Dubois siblings. "We're broke."

Of all the things Nyssa thought he might say, that was not one of them. She exchanged puzzled glances with her brother. "You're…broke? Whatever do you mean?"

"Our money. It's gone."

She blinked. All of the European royal families came from old money. They owned property and possessions worth millions, and the reigning monarchs received public subsidies. "I don't understand, Arthur. How can your money be gone?"

He tugged on the bottom of his shirt, clearly uncomfortable. "It's a long story."

"We'll make time to hear it."

Without being asked, John went over and picked up four chairs off one of the stacks surrounding them. Erik helped him flip them over, and the four of them sat closely together in a square. Nyssa took the seat opposite Arthur and gave him a smile. "Would you like a glass of schnapps, darling?"

Arthur let out a dry laugh. "Why not? Just don't let me near any fountains." His quip broke the tension and made them all smile.

John stood again. "Schnapps it is. I'll be right back." It only took a couple of minutes for him to return carrying a small silver tray with four glasses on it. Two contained schnapps, which he gave to Arthur and Erik. The glass of white wine he handed to Nyssa, and the tonic and lime he kept for himself. Technically, John was on the job even though he was attending tonight's ball as her date, so she wasn't surprised he'd decided to abstain from drinking alcohol.

She sipped her wine, pulling the hem of her ankle-length gown up a little so she was more comfortable. The four of them looked more like friends sitting around for an informal chat, rather than three royals and a bodyguard.

Arthur brought the glass John had handed him up to his lips and threw the alcohol down in one go, which made him cough and screw his face up. Erik looked like he wanted to say something, but Nyssa shook her head slightly and he closed his mouth again.

Once Arthur had downed his liquid courage, he began to explain. "Several years ago, Father began to make some investments. I warned him against doing so; it wasn't as though we needed the money, after all. But he met this man at an event who promised to double his investment, and after speaking with others decided to invest a lot of our money in a new start-up company, which was apparently making great strides in technology."

Nyssa's heart began to sink. She could already tell this was a story that didn't have a happy ending.

"This sounds vaguely familiar," Erik volunteered.

"Yes, it might. I believe my father spoke with yours about it, although Uncle Olivier was smart enough to decline the invitation to invest."

"Ah, that's why. Yes, I remember Papa mentioning it a few years back."

Arthur nodded. "Several others expressed some reservations about the whole thing, but Father was determined to go ahead against everyone's wishes, including Mother's. She's furious about the whole thing."

Nyssa moved to sit on the edge of her chair. "So what happened? The company failed?"

Arthur's hand squeezed the glass he was still holding. "The company never bloody existed in the first place. It was all a scam, a Ponzi scheme. This con artist has fleeced over a billion dollars all told. And that's only what we know of."

She gasped, her hand coming up to cover her mouth. "Oh, Arthur." She felt terrible for the man she sat opposite.

"Have the authorities been notified?"

John's question made Arthur snort. "Of course not. None of the royal families swindled in the scam want to involve the authorities."

"Because they're embarrassed," Nyssa explained quietly. "Surely they know they'll have to say something though."

"They'll have to speak up eventually, Arthur." This came from Erik. "It's possible the authorities could locate some of the stolen money and others need to be warned."

"I know all this, but Father is refusing to listen. Mother is so angry with him that she's threatened to leave him and go back to her family in France. If it were just me, I'd let him sort it out himself and move to London permanently, but the girls…"

Arthur had three younger sisters who were likely unaware of what was going on, and Nyssa knew he loved them enough to shield them from it. "I take it they don't know?"

"They suspect something is wrong, but they don't know what. The only reason I know is because Father has tasked me with trying to track down this con man and get the family's money returned."

"Oh, darling. How on earth does he think you're going to accomplish that?"

Arthur hung his head, his entire body sagging in the chair. "I don't know."

"Listen, mate. We can work something out if we put our heads together. Would you be willing to send me all the details you have to my private email?" Erik worked in finance, so she knew he might have some contacts he could tap privately for information.

"Your Highness, I have close friends who work for a private security company back in the U.S. called Centurion Security," John interjected. "They have contacts all over the world and some skilled IT experts working there, including forensic accountants. If you'd be willing to share what information you have, I can ask them to go digging. Quietly, of course. I can leave your name out of it."

Arthur's head snapped up. "You'd do that?"

"Of course. I'd be happy to help."

"Thank you." Arthur took a deep breath. "Thank you all. I'd really appreciate whatever assistance you can offer." He stood, glass still in hand, and they all rose up with him. John held out the silver tray he'd put on the floor, and they all placed their glasses on it. He disappeared out the door and returned a few moments later empty-handed.

Reaching into his pocket, he pulled out his wallet and extracted a business card. "This has my personal cell and email address on it." He handed it over to Arthur. "Feel free to contact me at any time."

The blond royal took the card and looked at the words printed on it carefully. "Thank you. I'll copy you in on the email to Erik so you have all the information I do." He held out his hand to John, who shook it. "You're a lucky man to have captured her heart." Arthur's gaze moved to Nyssa, who gave him a fond smile. "Take very good care of it."

"I will, promise."

John was not a man who made promises lightly, so hearing

him say that made warmth blossom in her chest. She stepped forward and embraced Arthur. "We'll do what we can to help, darling," she whispered in his ear. "You're not alone."

He pressed a kiss to her cheek. "I'm lucky to call you my friend. I'm sorry about springing marriage on you before. I really did think you knew about it." She hugged him tighter, letting him know she accepted his apology. "I would never hold you to it. I hope you know that."

"Of course I do," she whispered in his ear before releasing him.

Erik held out his hand, then pulled Arthur into a quick embrace before releasing him. "I'll come meet you in London week after next. We can go over everything you've learned together so I have a better understanding of what's going on."

John nodded. "I'd be happy to conference in from D.C. if that would help."

"Yes, splendid idea." Erik moved and clapped John on the back. "The more we know, the better." He headed for the door. "We'd better get back. Someone's likely to notice we're all missing."

Her brother was right. "Let's have another dance, Arthur. I'll be right out."

Arthur tilted his head, the corners of his mouth curling up ever so slightly before he followed Erik out the door, leaving Nyssa and John alone.

She stepped into his embrace, turning her face up for his kiss. "You're a good man, John Ashwood. You didn't have to offer any help." Her hands stroked his back underneath his jacket as he kissed her, his tongue sliding along hers.

When he finally let her go, he put the chairs back where he

got them from. “Of course I’ll help. He’s your friend.” They went to the door and slipped back out into the hallway. “We should get back inside. Arthur’s waiting for your dance.”

She got up on her toes and put her mouth next to his ear. “I’d much rather dance with you.”

“You will, later tonight. Wearing a lot less than you currently are.”

The idea of being naked again with the man she desperately loved made her shiver in anticipation. “I can’t wait.”

SEVEN

Nyssa

Nyssa was so distracted that the rest of the evening passed in a blur. She couldn't get what Arthur had revealed to her out of her head. She knew her parents and was sure they'd never force her to do something as life-altering as marry a man she didn't love, but she also knew Arthur had not made it up. He simply didn't have it in him to tell falsehoods about something so important.

She was also worried about the predicament Arthur's father had gotten their family into, although she knew that between Erik and John, Arthur had a good chance of finding out more information about the scammer who'd absconded with his family's millions.

She made a point of thanking the hosts of the event for their hospitality and congratulate them on such a successful evening, before saying goodnight to her family, Arabella, and Arthur. She promised the latter they'd speak more soon, and when he kissed her cheeks, he whispered in her ear not to worry too much because their families would come to some sort of agreement they could all live with.

Which only told her that despite what he'd said earlier on in the evening, he was hopeful she'd change her mind and agree to merge their families together through marriage…which would give Arthur and his family access to the Dubois family fortune.

She was numb to the cold as John walked her to their car, and murmured thanks as he held the door open for her, not closing it until she was completely settled and putting on her seat belt. He skirted around the front of the car before hopping into the driver's seat and starting both the engine and the heater.

They pulled out of the private parking lot and headed back to their hotel. She stared out the windshield, taking in the pedestrians hurrying down the street. Even though it was freezing outside, it was Saturday night and there was a good number of people to be seen.

"It's going to be okay, sweetheart." John's voice was deep and soft, and she reached across to place her hand on his thigh, comforted by being able to touch him. When they got to a red light, he took her hand in his and brought it up to his lips to kiss it.

Nyssa didn't answer, her brain swirling with all the conversations she'd had that night until her head started to hurt. She shivered, even though the interior of the car was warm, and when he raised her hand and kissed it again, she stroked his cheek gently with the backs of her fingers.

They'd get through this. She'd speak with her parents and make them see she loved John. Was in love with him. Wanted to marry and raise a family with him. She knew he'd stay by her side, as he had done for three years.

The rest of the ride went by in a blur. John parked the car in the spot they'd secured for the weekend beneath the hotel, then came around to open her door for her. She took his hand as she climbed out, and he kept hold of it as they headed for the private elevator that would take them to their floor.

She still hadn't uttered a word by the time John opened the

suite door and she stepped in behind him. He removed his coat and hung it up while Nyssa wandered over to the large floor-to-ceiling glass windows that gave her a perfect view of Paris sprawled below them at night. Hundreds of lights twinkled in the dark, but not even the sight of those could lift her spirits.

She felt him come up behind her, and when he wrapped his arms around her waist she leaned back against him, resting her hands on his. “Talk to me, Nyssa.”

Taking a few moments to collect her thoughts, she turned around to face him. “Arthur’s not lying.”

“I didn’t think he was.” John dipped his head and ran his nose down the side of hers before brushing a kiss across her lips. “Can your parents force you to marry him?”

She placed her hands on his arms, rubbing them up and down. “They would never force me, but they can…strongly recommend it.” He stilled, and had she not been gazing at him so closely she would have missed the tick in his jaw, which told her he was as unhappy about the situation as she was. She got up on her toes and pressed kisses to his face. “I won’t marry him, John. I don’t care what my parents say.”

By the time her lips kissed their way over to his, he’d pulled her closer so their bodies were pressed up against each other and she could feel every hard inch of him. Her hands came up to run through his hair as he slanted his mouth over hers in a long, deep kiss that took her breath away.

Tomorrow, they would talk with her parents about this agreement with Arthur’s family and she would make it clear no marriage would take place between the two royals. But for tonight, the only man Nyssa wanted to think about was the one holding her in his arms and sliding his tongue against hers.

When he finally let her go, his gaze traveled up and down her body slowly. "As beautiful as you are in this dress, I really fucking need you to take it off. Now."

Desire flared in his eyes as his tongue came out to lick his lips, and just like that she was wet for him. Her body burned for his touch. She ached to have him deep inside her, claiming her as no other man ever would. "You take it off me."

John wasted no time, moving his finger in a circle to encourage her to turn around. She did, and he unzipped the dress, exposing her naked back and the top of her red satin panties. She hadn't needed to wear a bra because the dress had one built in, and she'd bought the panties on a whim just before they'd left D.C.

She turned back around, holding the dress up in front of her chest. The naked, raw look in his eyes told her he appreciated her recent purchase. With a smile, she dropped the dress and stepped out of it, leaving her clad only in her panties and heels.

He bent over and picked the dress up before placing it carefully over the back of a chair nearby, while she took off her jewelry. Removing the pins keeping her tiara in place, she carefully lifted the expensive headpiece off the crown of her head and locked them all away in the special case they'd been stored in for the trip.

Going back over to where John stood, she watched as he picked up the remote to close the blinds, then started to remove his own clothing. She grew wetter as naked skin appeared in view, the hard lines and edges of his body showcasing his muscles nicely. Dark hair lightly covered his chest, and once he removed his underwear, she could see how it grew coarser as it trailed down his stomach to surround his long, thick cock, which was already hard.

She hadn't realized she'd let out a moan until he'd closed the distance between them to kiss her. She managed to kick off her shoes as his hands slid inside the back of her panties to grab her ass and squeeze it while his tongue played with hers. Her nipples were hard and aching for his mouth, and if he didn't slide inside her soon, she'd combust with need.

"John." His name was a plea and if the look on his face was anything to go by, he'd heard and understood it.

"I know what you need, sweetheart. You need me to suck on these gorgeous tits of yours, make your nipples all nice and hard. You need me to lick your sweet pussy and make you come on my tongue, and you need me to fuck you so hard you'll be walking funny tomorrow."

She gasped, his dirty mouth making her burn for it all. For him. She nodded, unable to speak anymore, and didn't utter a murmur of protest when he swept her into his arms and carried her into the bedroom, placing her gently on the bed. She pushed the pillows on one side off the bed and moved the others across to the middle, then got comfortable and waited.

The man she loved was standing at the foot of the bed, gazing at her naked beauty. Then he got onto it and crawled toward her until he was kneeling in between her spread thighs. He tugged on her panties. "These need to come off." Nyssa raised her legs up and straightened them before lifting her hips so he could pull them off her. Throwing them onto the floor, John waited until she'd brought her legs back down then spread them wide and settled down on his stomach in between them.

She let out a moan at the feel of his tongue swiping through her pussy, then cried out when he latched on to her clit and sucked it lightly, her hips bucking. Her fingers grasped his neatly styled dark brown hair as his tongue licked and swirled. When one finger slid inside her, she was wet and ready for him. He added another, then crooked them in just the right spot.

To her surprise, she came instantly with a sharp cry, her hips rising and his tongue still licking her clit. White-hot pleasure speared through her and she tightened her grip on her lover's hair as she floated back down in a state of bliss.

Breathing heavily, she felt his fingers withdraw and managed to find enough energy to sit up on her elbows. John was still nestled between her legs, the corners of his mouth curled up in a smug grin. "You okay?"

She took a few deep breaths before answering, "I'm not sure I'll be able to move again for a long while." He laughed as he rose above her, covering her body with his and coaxing her to lie back down. She did, her hands roaming over his warm, naked skin, caressing his back and then drifting down to cup his firm ass and squeeze it gently. "Mine."

He gazed down at her, his gorgeous blue eyes wide and shining with love. "Yours."

Bracing his weight on his arms, he kissed her softly. It soon grew heated as their tongues met and explored. Nyssa eventually pulled away, gasping for air. "John." His name was a plea on her lips, one he acknowledged with a nod.

Settling himself between her legs and spreading them farther, he reached down and grabbed his cock, sliding the head of it through the folds of her pussy before slipping it into her entrance. "Look at me, Nyssa. Look at me while I ruin you for any other man."

She couldn't take her eyes off him as he slid balls deep

inside her in one smooth stroke. Transfixed by the look of concentration on his face, she brought one hand up to cup his cheek as he pulled out and drove back into her over and over. Cries of pleasure spilled from her lips at how well he filled her, stretched her open to take his long, thick cock.

"That's my good girl," he crooned. "Look at you taking my cock so well." He kissed her then, timing the strokes of his tongue against hers to match the thrust of his cock in her pussy.

She raised her hips to meet his, wanting him as deeply as possible inside her. All of a sudden, he pulled out and got up on his knees. When she let out a wail at the loss, he grinned. "Get up on your hands and knees, my princess."

He held out his hands and she took them, allowing him to pull her up so she was kneeling. But before she turned around, she smiled at him cheekily and then dipped her head to run her tongue from the base of his cock to the top, making him groan loudly. "Fuck." She went to do it again, but he grabbed her arms gently. "Later. Turn around, Nyssa. I need to fuck your pussy right now."

She did as she was told, getting on her hands and knees in front of him and opening her legs far enough for him to kneel between them. He grabbed her hips and eased her back onto his cock, and she was so wet he slid in up to the hilt in one easy thrust.

Her cries were loud as he pounded into her, and she let her head fall forward when he reached around to cup her breasts and play with her nipples. It was almost too much. Too much stimulation, too much pleasure.

Her second orgasm of the night slammed into her as suddenly as the first one had, and she let out a wail as her body trembled. John pushed in once more and stopped moving, obviously enjoying the way she clenched and fluttered around his cock if the moan he let loose was anything to go by. “That’s it, sweetheart. I love when you come all over my cock.”

Once she stopped shaking, she slumped her torso on the bed and stretched her arms in front of her, grabbing the covers and clutching them. Her ass was still in the air, and soon enough he began to move inside her again. It wasn’t long before he slammed into her one final time and she felt the heat of his orgasm deep within her.

EIGHT

Nyssa

Nyssa took a deep breath as she placed one hand on the door to the suite where she was having brunch with her parents and brother. The other was firmly entwined with John's, and he squeezed it reassuringly.

"We don't have to tell them now if you're not ready, sweetheart. I don't mind waiting."

She turned to him, taking his free hand in hers. "I don't want to wait any longer, John. I want them to know we're in love and you'll be joining the family." She paused, tilting her head to the side. "You do realize if we marry that will make you a prince?"

His eyes widened just a little, then the surprised expression was gone in an instant. He leaned down and nuzzled her neck. "You mean when we marry, right?"

She couldn't stop the corners of her mouth turning up in a huge grin. "Right."

When his lips met hers, she was in no rush to let him go. She let all her worries float away and concentrated on kissing the man she was madly in love with. Eventually, they parted and she straightened her back and shoulders. "Let's do this."

John released her hand and knocked on the large wooden door before pushing it open. He stepped into the room ahead of her and held the door open.

"Good morning, darling." Her parents and brother were

already at the table, and they rose to greet the new arrivals.

"Good morning, Maman." Nyssa kissed her mother's cheeks and gave her a warm hug, before bestowing the same greeting on her father and brother.

John hovered behind her, waiting until she'd finished before he bowed in front of the royal family. "Good morning, Your Majesties." He turned to Erik. "Your Highness."

Erik waved at him. "You know you don't have to stand on ceremony when we're in private, John. Erik is just fine."

The queen held out her hands to Nyssa's lover, and he took them before leaning down to kiss each cheek in greeting before shaking the king's and prince's hands. "You're very welcome to call us Manon and Olivier in private, John," the queen invited. "After all, if I'm not mistaken you'll be joining the family soon enough." Her gaze shifted to her daughter, one perfectly sculpted eyebrow arched in question.

Nyssa gave her mother a warm smile. "Come, let's sit and talk." The private butler assigned to the monarchs' suite served them hot beverages in expensive china before slipping out of the room once more.

Once they'd all make their teas and coffees to their liking, Nyssa took a deep breath before gazing at her parents. She felt John's hand on her thigh, and his touch both relaxed and reassured her. "Maman, Papa, John and I have recently begun a romantic relationship."

Her father's face went blank and he looked directly at John. Nyssa had seen many a person on the receiving end of such a stare, and she frowned. "Papa, stop it."

The older man suddenly burst into laughter after her mother swiped his arm. "Olivier, don't make John uncomfortable," the queen scolded him. She then turned toward her daughter. "We're very happy for you both, darling. We know John is a good man and if he makes you happy, that's all that matters to us."

"Your Majesties, I assure you this is not some passing fancy for me. I'm very much in love with your daughter and want to spend the rest of my life by her side, if she'll have me." He lifted their joined hands up to his lips and pressed a kiss to the back of hers.

She blinked back a few tears. "You know I will."

"Arthur will be most disappointed to hear that." Her brother's dry, droll tone interrupted the moment, and her mother laughed.

But Nyssa realized he'd given her the perfect opening to question her parents. "Speaking of Arthur," she began delicately, placing her cup of coffee down on the table, "he told me something last night that was quite startling."

"Oh?" Olivier looked at her questioningly. "What was that?"

She gazed at her parents, who were seated across the table from her. "He told me our parents had made some sort of agreement when we were children that should we both reach the age of thirty and remain unmarried, we would marry each other to strengthen the relations between our two countries."

Her parents had very different reactions. Her mother laughed, obviously amused by such a notion, but her father stilled in his seat, going pale. "Oh, darling. I have no idea why on earth Arthur would have made up such a ridiculous thing. Ignore him." This came from her mother, who was still smiling as she sipped her tea.

Nyssa frowned as she took in her father's appearance. "Papa? Is he telling the truth?"

She already knew the answer deep down, but she needed her father to confirm it. Her heart was heavy when he nodded once. "Yes, he's telling the truth."

The smile slipped off her mother's face and it was clear she knew nothing about it. "What? Olivier, what are you talking about?"

"It was a very long time ago. George and I were…well, let's just say we'd had some drinks and since Nyssa and Arthur are around the same age, it seemed like a good idea at the time."

"Olivier!"

"You don't have to worry, my dear." He reached over and patted his daughter's hand. "Nobody is going to force you to marry Arthur. I'm surprised George even told his son about it."

"Good," Nyssa exclaimed, relief washing over her. "There's only one man I want to marry, and he's sitting in this room with us."

John squeezed her hand again and she gave him a warm smile before breaking protocol and leaning over to press a soft kiss to his lips.

"You and I will discuss this later." The queen's tone made it clear she was not happy with her husband, and Erik gave an exaggerated wince.

"Uh oh. Someone's in the doghouse."

Nyssa couldn't help but laugh at her brother's comment, and she covered it up with a fake cough. Even the family's dogs had luxurious dwellings, and the thought of her father being banished to one amused her no end.

The food was brought to the table by several waiters, and the spread was appropriately fit for royalty. There was a platter of fresh fruit, along with another full of pastries such as croissants, brioche, and pain au chocolat, Nyssa's favorite. The hot food consisted of scrambled eggs, smoked salmon, bacon, and a quiche which smelled delicious.

Once everyone had laden their plates, they chatted about the success of the previous night's ball, and Nyssa was delighted to learn her father had won one of the silent auctions—a week-long trip to a private resort in Switzerland for two. "Your mother and I thought you and John might enjoy it."

"It sounds wonderful, Papa! Thank you. I'm not sure when we could go because the next few months are incredibly busy for us, but perhaps in the autumn."

Discussion then turned to Nyssa's job as their country's ambassador, and she brought her family up to date with the latest news. They all spoke in a video call once a week to discuss things, but it was still nice to talk in person.

They spent several hours with her family, and her heart warmed to see them include John in their conversation as much as possible. They didn't feel the need to censor anything, since John was privy to a lot of the royal family's private information as necessary in his role. Her father occasionally lapsed into French, the national language of Lecroisa, but her mother always reminded him John was not fluent in French and he switched back to English with an apology.

Her parents had accepted their relationship as easily as her brother had, and not for the first time Nyssa was so grateful to have the wonderful family she did. She enjoyed every moment of their company, but eventually they said their goodbyes. Her family was flying back home that evening, while Nyssa and John would depart the French capital the following morning. While she was glad to have a final evening in one of her favorite cities in the world, she wished she could have a little more time with her loved ones.

After farewelling them with hugs and kisses so they could pack and head to the airport, Nyssa and John went back to their suite. A lot of stores were closed on Sunday afternoons in Paris, although tourist areas would remain open, so given the cold weather they opted to stay indoors.

It didn't take much coaxing from John for Nyssa to remove her clothes, and she was rewarded with a couple of orgasms. One of which left her gasping for air while bent over the expensive cream sofa while clutching one of the mint green and gold cushions on it, his cock sliding deep inside her as he came just after she did.

After taking a long, hot shower together, in which they washed each other reverently, their hands exploring each other's bodies, they redressed and watched a little television.

"Shall we order in tonight?" She was curled up against him, his arms around her, and she brushed her lips against his jaw.

"We can do that, but we're going out after dinner."

That made Nyssa sit up. "We are? Where?"

He gave her a mysterious grin. "It's a surprise."

"What? No! You have to tell me."

"No, I don't." John laughed and tugged her down for a kiss. She got lost in the feel of his mouth on hers, his tongue demanding entry, and by the time he let her go all thoughts had drifted out of her head.

She settled back down next to him, and later on they ordered dinner. Once their plates were empty, they dressed warmly to venture out in the winter night and headed for their car.

Nyssa recognized where John was driving them to: the Eiffel

Tower. But why? They'd both visited it on their last trip to Paris eighteen months previously, although admittedly it hadn't been at nighttime. It didn't matter though; she couldn't get enough of the amazing views from the top. The Louvre, Champs Elysees, the Seine River, and the Grand Palace were just a few of the Parisian landmarks visible from the peak and she knew they'd look majestic in the night lights.

It was a short walk from where they parked the car, and she clung to his gloved hand as they wandered through the night to their destination.

NINE

Nyssa

Despite the fact it was incredibly cold, there were dozens of people milling around the gardens at the base of the Eiffel Tower when they arrived, taking photos and marveling at the tall structure towering above their heads. Yet others were making their way to the elevators, which would transport them high above the ground to be treated to a view like no other.

Nyssa had been prepared to join the other tourists and wait in line—possible since she was rarely recognized when out in public, even in Europe—but John led her to an elevator with no line. She squeezed the hand holding hers. "Where are we going?"

He turned to look at her and gave her the grin which always both melted her heart and made her wet with desire. "You'll see." He brought their joined hands up to his mouth and pressed a kiss to the back of her glove.

Curious, she followed him without question. When they got close to the door, a tall, slim man with thinning gray hair was waiting for them. He bowed in front of Nyssa. "Bonsoir Votre Altesse." *Good evening, Your Highness*. He then accepted John's outstretched hand. "Mr. Ashwood. Please follow me."

They stepped into the elevator and were whisked high above the ground at an almost dizzying pace. Nyssa snuggled into John, who tucked her underneath his arm and pressed a kiss to her temple. She stared out the window, watching as the ground became smaller and the people walking around on it began to resemble ants.

When they reached their destination, they stepped out of the elevator and into a warm, empty room. Nobody was present except the three of them. "It's my pleasure to welcome you to a private tour of the Eiffel Tower this evening. My name is Pierre and I'll be happy to answer any questions you may have. Would you both like a drink?"

"Oui, s'il vous plait." *Yes, please*. Nyssa gave him a bright smile and accepted the glass of champagne their host offered. They chatted for several minutes, Pierre demonstrating a knowledge of Nyssa's country she had not been expecting. He'd obviously done his research, which she appreciated. Once they were finished drinking, they left their glasses on the table and followed him to a staircase which led them to the top of the Eiffel Tower.

The private viewing platform they stood on was out in the open, meaning the icy wind had them shivering, but the view was unbeatable. Nyssa gazed down at the city spread open before them. Lights adorned the various landmarks, easy to make out even in the dark. The Arc de Triomphe. The Louvre. Notre Dame Cathedral, which was still being rebuilt after the terrible fire which destroyed much of it several years previously.

They walked around the entire length of the platform, which wrapped around the tower, and soaked it all in. "Paris is such a beautiful city." Her tone was a little wistful. She'd spent several months living in Paris when she'd been younger, and part of her wished she still resided there.

"It sure is." John was standing behind her, his arms around

her waist, his warmth seeping into her despite the frigid weather. "But the most beautiful thing in it is standing in my arms right now."

She glanced around, only to discover Pierre had discreetly disappeared to give them some privacy. Pivoting in his arms, she moved so she could face her lover. "John?"

"Hmm?"

"I love you." Her voice was barely above a whisper, but his face was so close to hers she didn't need to raise it for him to hear her.

"Je t'aime aussi, ma princesse." *I love you too, my princess*. He dipped his head and closed the distance between them, his lips pressing against hers. They were cold for a moment, but soon enough all she felt was the heat between them.

He slid his tongue into her mouth and explored it thoroughly, and by the time he let her go she'd forgotten where they were for a few moments. Resting his forehead on hers, the corners of his mouth turned up. "I'm almost sorry we're flying out tomorrow morning."

"So am I," she agreed. "But maybe we can come back for a holiday soon?"

"That sounds like an excellent idea. Perhaps in the late spring, when it will be warmer."

"What about for your birthday?" Nyssa knew his birthday was in late May, and spending a week in Paris would be a wonderful way to celebrate. Her mind ticked over as she began to think of all the things they could do and see and explore.

"Sounds like a plan." He kissed her again, then moved back just far enough for her to be able to turn back around and look out over the city.

They stared down at the lights blanketing Paris, walking hand in hand around the platform and pointing out various sites to each other. When they got back around to the stairs they'd come up, Pierre was waiting for them, seemingly stepping out of the dark. "Beautiful up here, isn't it?"

"Absolutely," Nyssa agreed. "But I think we're ready to go back inside and get out of the cold."

"Of course. Please follow me." He led them back down the small spiral staircase and into the room they first stepped into. He poured them both another glass of expensive champagne and encouraged them to help themselves to the chocolate-covered strawberries which had appeared on the table in their absence.

Once they were done imbibing, their host handed John a small device with a large red button in the middle of it. Like smoke, he once again made himself scarce as John handed the device to Nyssa. "I've made arrangements for you to do something very special tonight."

Her brows furrowed. "Something special?"

He glanced at his watch. "If you press the button in exactly one minute, something will happen. Come watch."

He led her over to a small television screen she hadn't even noticed, and like magic it turned on and a picture of the Eiffel Tower appeared on it. The camera was level with the ground, angled upward to take the entire tower in frame. "What now?"

John looked at his watch again. "Okay, get ready to press the button in ten, nine, eight…." Once he'd counted down to one, Nyssa pressed the button and looked at the screen.

All of a sudden, the lights on the Eiffel Tower began to sparkle. After placing the box down on the table nearest her, she watched, mesmerized, as the tower shimmered in the dark for a full five minutes before the sparkling stopped. With a grin, she turned to the man by her side. "I didn't do that." She knew very well the lights sparkled for five minutes every hour automatically after dusk until 11:00 p.m., but she appreciated the gesture anyway.

"Sure you did. You always light up my life."

She kissed him, a soft, gentle kiss full of love. "I had no idea you're such a romantic."

He grunted. "Must be the city."

Her laugh echoed throughout the room. Pierre stepped back into it from a door she hadn't even realized existed and approached them both, a small, white box tied with a red ribbon in hand. "Please feel free to stay here as long as you wish. The elevator will take you back down to the ground when you're ready. I'm glad you were able to explore the Eiffel Tower, and I leave you with this gift. Good evening." With a bow, he left them alone.

Nyssa undid the ribbon and removed the lid of the box. Inside, she discovered what looked like a screw with an extended base. "What is this?"

"It's a rivet." John picked it up and showed her the number stamped into it. "It's one of the millions of rivets that was used in the construction of the tower. It's since been replaced, but now you can say you own a part of the Eiffel Tower."

It was such an unusual yet thoughtful gift, and she loved it. "Merci, mon amour." *Thank you, my love*. She planned to place it somewhere of prominence in her home back in D.C. In what she hoped would become their home.

She didn't voice her thoughts in the car on the way back to the hotel, instead choosing to gaze out the window and enjoy the night lights of Paris one final time before they left. She knew they'd come back to Paris again and again, so her heart was light instead of being sad they would be leaving soon.

They drove back to the hotel in comfortable silence, then removed their outer clothing once safely back in their suite. She knew from the text message waiting for her from her brother that her family was now safely back in Lecroisa. After responding to let him know she'd text him the following day when she and John were back in America, she turned her phone on to vibrate only, wanting to devote all her attention to one man.

TEN
John

Although it was late and they had an early flight back to D.C. the following morning, John wasn't tired and he didn't think the beautiful princess he loved was either. So he suggested they take a bath together, because the bathroom in their suite was nothing short of spectacular and he wanted to enjoy it before they left Paris.

Nyssa was clearly on board with the idea if the way she raced to the bathroom was any indication. He trailed behind her, mesmerized as he watched pieces of her clothing appear on the floor, leaving a trail for him to follow. By the time he got to the bathroom, the water was already running and he'd stripped down to his pants.

He glanced around the large room. The walls, cabinets, and floors were all made of the same cream marble and all the hardware was gold. Two sinks graced the middle of the large vanity, which took up one entire wall. Each sink had its own mirror and three-shelf display. Numerous bunches of white flowers dotted the room, as did groups of two and three candles. The three large ones sitting in a corner of the bath had already been lit, but the rose scent wasn't overpowering. Towels had been carefully placed in the opposite corner.

As luxurious as the bathroom was, John couldn't tear his gaze from the woman standing next to the tub. Nyssa leaned over to test the temperature of the water before she nodded once and shut the faucet off. Bubbles covered the surface of the water, and a pillow sat down at one end.

She was clad only in pastel pink lingerie that hid nothing. He could see her hardened nipples poking through the lace of her bra, and her dark curls were visible through her panties. "Take them off." His voice was deep, hoarse, and he watched silently as Nyssa removed the remainder of her clothing, leaving her standing in front of him, bared to his hungry gaze. "Fuck, you're beautiful."

The smile she gave him was almost shy, but the way her nipples tightened told a different story. "You seem to have too much clothing on, Mr. Ashwood."

He leaned over and kissed her, enjoying the feel of her warm, soft lips on his. "Let me fix that."

He stripped as quickly as possible, his dick already hard and pointing directly at her. Nyssa raised an eyebrow, the corners of her mouth curling up. "Is that for me?"

"Always for you. Only for you."

She wrapped a hand around the base of his cock and gave it a slow, hard stroke. Her thumb swiped across the head, making him hiss, before she continued to trail her fingers over his sensitive flesh. Then without warning, she perched on the edge of the bathtub and leaned over, flicking her tongue over the crown of his cock.

"Fuck."

Glancing up at him, she smiled, then wrapped her hand back around the base of his cock and sucked the tip into her mouth. Her free hand came down to cup his balls and play with them while she sucked his dick, her cheeks hollowing as she ran her tongue up the underside of it. He closed his eyes and let his head fall back, the wet suction of her mouth and the tickling of his balls making him so hard he could pound nails.

When he was getting dangerously close to coming, he opened his eyes again and looked down at his woman. “Enough, Nyssa.” He helped her back to her feet, then waited until she’d pinned her hair up off her face. Holding out his hand, she took it and stepped up into the opulent bathtub.

He climbed in behind her and sat down, leaning against the back of the tub and placing the pillow underneath his neck to soften the hard edges of the marble. She waited until he was comfortable before she seated herself in front of him, leaning back against him.

John wrapped his arms around her, their naked bodies now floating in bubbles. He trailed his lips across her shoulder and up her neck, pressing them against her soft, warm skin. He would never tire of this. Never tire of holding the woman he was madly in love with in his embrace. Showing her without words how deeply his love for her ran.

She giggled when his lips brushed her ear, a place he’d learned she was ticklish. He kept going, gliding across her jaw and cheek, until his mouth slanted over hers and he slid his tongue inside. Her kisses were as enthusiastic as his, and he loved it.

Loved her so much.

Eventually, he released her mouth and simply lay back to enjoy the feel of her body against his. His fingers trailed down her stomach, where he paused to place his hand over it. He could see it in his mind’s eye, big and round and full, and he was going to make that happen one day. He couldn’t wait to fuck his baby into her. She was going to be an amazing mother: loving, warm, caring, and protective.

But for now, he was going to enjoy her as much and as often as possible.

Her hand was curled around his arm as she moved it slowly up and down. “Back to reality tomorrow.” She let out a small sigh, and he understood.

“Nothing changes between us, sweetheart. I’m still going to love you tomorrow.”

She turned her head to look at him, her eyes shining. “Promise?”

“I promise.” He kissed her, then ran his nose up the side of hers before kissing her again. She relaxed once more, and they sat together in the dim light in companionable silence. “We need to talk about the job though.”

“The job?”

“I can’t be your bodyguard anymore, Nyssa. I’m no longer objective.”

She turned her head and gazed at him, her warm brown eyes wide and alert. “Have you been totally objective the last two years, knowing how you felt about me?”

He knew she was right to call him on his bullshit. There wasn’t any reason he couldn’t retain the role he’d been employed in for the last three years. Nyssa would still need someone to do everything he did, and there was no way he was going to allow another man to spend so much time with his lover. But he’d had to make the offer anyway.

“Not the point. I can’t hide how I feel about you any longer, and I don’t fucking want to.”

Her lips brushed his cheek. “So don’t. You can still do the

job, John. You'll just be doing it as my partner now."

He cupped her breasts and played with her nipples as he kissed her mouth thoroughly until she was panting. "And then as your husband, as soon as I can manage it." She nodded, her eyes alight with desire. "Stand up and bend over."

Her soft gasp echoed around the quiet room. "What?"

"Up. I need to taste you right fucking now." He grabbed her hips and propelled her upward until she was standing right in front of him. "Bend over, sweetheart, and open your legs."

He knew she was probably feeling a little exposed. The physical part of their relationship was still new, but she'd get used to it. Get used to him wanting to feast on her sweet pussy. He sat up and waited until she was bent at the waist in front of him and he was eye level with the part of her he craved the most.

After lightly smacking her ass, which caused her to let out a surprised moan, he spread her open with his fingers and ran his tongue from her clit to her opening. He lapped at her, licking up and down, circling her clit before flicking his tongue across it. The way she moved her hips and her ever-growing cries of pleasure told him she was enjoying his attention as much as he was.

He added some fingers to the mix, and it wasn't long before she climaxed. He licked her clean, then rose up out of the water, bubbles clinging to his skin. Standing behind her, he stroked his cock a few times before grabbing her by the hips and easing the head of his dick inside her.

Nyssa dropped her head forward as she moaned and pushed back against him, inching him farther inside. He stopped moving and looked at the mirror in front of them, entranced by the picture they presented. "Look up, Nyssa."

Once she did, he caught her gaze in their reflection and watched her face as he pushed into her, not stopping until he was balls deep. Fuck. She was so wet. So fucking *tight*. If he wasn't careful, he was going to come like a schoolboy looking at a pair of tits for the first time. Her body trembled as he remained still, enjoying the feel of his dick so deep inside her.

"John." Her voice was shaky, her grip on the edge of the bath turning her knuckles white. "I need you to move, sweetheart."

He did. Slow, deep strokes at first, until he couldn't go slow anymore and his thrusts became hard and fast. Her cries were loud as she encouraged him to keep going, to make her come again. He did just that, only barely able to hold on until she shuddered as she orgasmed and screamed.

He followed her into the abyss, white-hot pleasure zinging through him like lightning as he held her steady and spilled his release in her womb with a long, loud groan.

Fuck. Would sex with Nyssa always be this good? He sure hoped so.

By the time they were done, the water had cooled and they still had to pack, so after John grabbed a washcloth and wiped away the evidence of their lovemaking, he helped Nyssa out of the tub. Grabbing a towel, he dried her first, then himself with the other she'd neatly placed in the corner. She blew out the candles and he helped her into one of the fluffy white robes that probably cost a thousand euro to take home.

Once they were both covered, they wandered into the bedroom. John pulled out their suitcases while Nyssa started folding everything neatly and packing them away. Since they'd both traveled extensively in the past, it didn't take long for all their possessions to be packed in preparation for their morning flight.

After they were done, they fell into bed. He made sure she was comfortable before turning out the lights and setting an alarm on his phone, although he was sure it wouldn't be needed. Military life meant he always rose early, even on weekends. If they woke early enough, perhaps they could have a bite to eat and make love one more time before they left Paris to head back to the States.

To their new life together. A life that had begun there in Paris over the course of one weekend but would last for the rest of their lives.

ELEVEN

Nyssa

Nyssa took her seat near the window on the private plane that belonged to the Dubois family. They were wealthy enough to have a couple at their disposal when required, but Nyssa had been allocated one permanently when she'd moved to the U.S. as Lecroisa's ambassador. Traveling was something that was part of her position, and her family refused to let her fly on commercial airlines as a safety precaution.

The interior of the plane was opulent without being too gaudy. The wide seats were made of cream leather, and good quality pillows and cashmere blankets were readily available. The plane had internet capability and each seat had its own entertainment unit with thousands of shows and movies available to watch.

She was grateful for the luxurious ride back to Washington because she was tired. Sleep was not a commodity she'd had a lot of while in Paris, although she wasn't complaining about the reason why. She wouldn't have traded anything for this weekend with John, but knowing there was a bedroom on the plane where they could rest was a relief.

She hadn't bothered with a flight attendant since they were perfectly capable of serving themselves. They'd eaten an early breakfast at the hotel, and John had dashed out to a nearby boulangerie to grab some pastries for the flight before they'd left. Once the pilots checked they were ready to depart Paris, they settled into their seats for the journey, which would take a little over eight and a half hours and get them back to Washington about midday local time.

Once the plane had leveled out and the seat belt sign had been turned off, they both got up and went into the kitchen to grab drinks and snacks. Nyssa opted for an orange juice while John went for a Coke, and they shared the pastries he'd picked up.

It didn't take them long to consume everything, and for a little while they held hands in companionable silence. "Are you tired, sweetheart?"

John's question had her looking over at him. He looked as tired as she felt, and a nap was just the thing they both needed. "I am. Shall we get some sleep?"

They stood and took their trash to the kitchen. John let the pilots know they were going to rest for a few hours so they wouldn't be disturbed, then headed back to the bedroom located toward the tail of the plane. Once he'd closed the door behind them, Nyssa removed her warm sweater.

"You want to join the Mile High Club?"

She spun around to see a devious grin on her lover's handsome face and decided to tease him a little. "What makes you think I'm not already in it?"

The surprised look he gave her told her he'd not been expecting that response, and she had to fight to stop the burst of laughter bubbling up inside from coming out. "Seriously? You've had sex on a plane before?"

"No. I'm only teasing you." She did laugh now, and the growl he let out made her laugh even harder.

"You're going to pay for that. You're laughing now, but soon enough you'll be screaming."

The look of raw hunger on his face as his gaze raked over her body made her shiver in anticipation. "Don't make promises you can't keep, Ashwood." She kept her tone light and flirty, and when their eyes met, she was wet and ready for him. Judging by the large bulge pressing against the zipper of his jeans, he was equally as aroused.

He crossed over to close the distance between them and pulled on the zipper of her black jeans before yanking them down her legs. After helping her remove her boots and socks, he pulled the jeans off while she removed the tee she'd been wearing underneath her sweater.

When he slid her panties down and pressed a kiss to the dark, damp curls between her thighs before breathing in her scent, she let out a soft moan. As he kissed his way up her body, she removed her bra so she was standing bare before him. She was rewarded by the feel of his mouth wrapping around one nipple and tugging on it lightly with his teeth, before he released it, laving it with his tongue until it was hard and aching.

He then did the same to her other nipple as she pulled his sweater and Henley up over his head. He kicked off his sneakers and socks, then removed his jeans and boxer briefs. Nyssa watched as his long, hard cock smacked his stomach before jutting out from a nest of dark curls toward her.

She couldn't help it. She sat on the edge of the bed and wrapped her hand around the base of his cock before sucking it deep into her mouth, hollowing her cheeks and running her tongue up the underside of it.

"Fuck." One hand came to tangle in her hair as she bobbed

up and down, taking him as deeply as she could. She glanced up to see his head was back, eyes closed and mouth open in ecstasy. Nyssa felt so powerful at that moment, seeing the strong, capable man she loved so lost in what she was doing to him.

She ran her tongue over the head of his cock, lapping up his arousal. He groaned even more loudly before his eyes snapped open. “Enough.”

He pulled her gently to her feet, then turned her around and pushed down on her spine, indicating for her to bend over in front of him. She did so without resistance and soon enough she felt the head of his cock tunneling through her folds to slip inside her. With one hard shove, he impaled her on his dick.

She cried out and pushed back against him, taking him a little deeper and bracing herself on her hands, which were pressed firmly on the bed. She whimpered his name, and his hips began to move.

His cock pistoned in and out of her, his balls slapping against her clit, making her so wet he was able to glide inside her body easily. “Holy fuck, Nyssa. Your pussy’s so fucking tight, baby.”

She lifted her left leg up and placed her foot on the edge of the bed, opening herself up to him farther, and he rewarded her with a few hard, deep thrusts that had her seeing stars and crying out with every motion. She orgasmed in a ridiculously short amount of time, clenching down hard on him, which in turn caused him to slam into her one last time and detonate inside her.

Once he eventually withdrew from her body, she crawled onto the bed and flopped down, her heart still racing and her legs trembling from the force of their orgasms. The bed dipped behind her, and then she felt a finger trailing up the back of her leg from her ankle to her ass. John cupped it and squeezed gently, then a few moments later she felt his lips pressing a soft kiss there. He then climbed over her and lay down on his back, his eyes closed and one hand resting on her behind.

She pressed a kiss to his shoulder. "Come on, let's get into bed properly and get some sleep. I'm exhausted."

They managed to find the energy to climb under the covers and curl up together. She rested her head on his shoulder as he held her close. "John?"

"Yes, sweetheart?"

"Will you move in with me when we get back to D.C.?"

He raised an eyebrow. "I already live with you."

She swatted his shoulder playfully. "In the guesthouse. I'm talking about you moving into the main house. Sleeping in the same bed as me every night."

"Hmm." He tapped his lips with one finger as though giving it serious thought, and then what he said next shocked her. "No, I don't think I want to move into the house as your boyfriend." He suddenly climbed back out of the bed and padded over to where his jeans lay on the floor, tossed haphazardly in his quest to get naked. He reached into a front pocket, then came back to bed, sitting up.

She did the same, covering her breasts with the sheet as she gazed at him. "You don't want to move in with me?"

"Not as your boyfriend, no." He opened his clenched hand to reveal a beautiful ring. Nyssa gasped and let go of her grip on the sheet as she gazed at the piece of jewelry. A large, round blue stone which matched the color of his eyes sat in the middle of the solid yellow gold band, with white diamonds inlaid on either side. "But I'd love to move in as your fiancé."

She looked up at him through tears. “John.”

“Will you marry me, Nyssa? Make me the luckiest man on the planet and be my wife?”

“Yes! I’d love to marry you.” She was nodding as she lifted her left hand up and he slid the ring on her finger. Nyssa stared at it, gobsmacked at how beautiful it was. She gazed at the center stone, entranced by the color.

“It’s a blue diamond,” he explained. “They’re rare and beautiful. Just like you.”

“I love it.” That was true; she couldn’t have picked better herself. Leaning in, she kissed him slowly, thoroughly, and he pulled her onto his lap, holding her close.

They only parted to suck in some air, and Nyssa stared down at her engagement ring once more. “I can’t wait to be your wife.”

He placed a hand underneath her chin and tipped it up so she was looking directly into his eyes. “I can’t wait to be your husband, Mrs. Ashwood.” She grinned as he kissed her again, then they settled down in each other’s embrace as they flew high above the ground toward a new life together.

Thank you so much for reading ONE WEEKEND IN PARIS! I hope you enjoyed Nyssa and John's story and I'd love it if you would consider leaving a review or sending me a message to let me know. I always love hearing from my readers.

John mentioned CENTURION SECURITY in this book. It's the name of my forthcoming romantic suspense series, so be sure to sign up for my newsletter and follow me on social media so you don't miss out on any bookish news: https://www.lissannejones.com/newsletter

Want to read some more novellas set over the course of a weekend in various locations around the world? I'm fortunate enough to be joined by dozens of other amazing romance authors for this series! You can find all the details on the One Weekend page on my website: https://www.lissannejones.com/oneweekend

ACKNOWLEDGEMENTS

Quite some time ago, I had an idea of writing a series of novellas all set over the course of one weekend in locations all over the globe. Eventually, I came to realize I simply didn't have the time to write them all myself, so I asked if there were any other authors who liked the idea enough to want to write a book (or two!) with me.

To my surprise, there were plenty! Thank you so much to all the wonderful authors who are also writing a One Weekend novella for doing this series with me. I do hope you'll check out their books as well. I can't wait to read them.

Big thanks go to my amazing editing and beta team: Karen Hrdlicka, Kari Wolff, Tracey Wilson-Vuolo, and Anna del Mar. I couldn't do this without you!

Thank you so much to the talented Kim Wilson for designing all the One Weekend covers. They're stunning and are going to look so good on my bookshelf.

Thanks go to Alexandra Silva for being there for me behind the scenes as I launched this series, and for creating the most gorgeous teasers about Nyssa and John for me. I'm grateful for your support and generosity.

My thanks go to Chelsea West for reading over the manuscript and checking my French translations were correct. I appreciate you taking the time to proofread it for me.

Thank you to Lou Stock for doing the incredible interior formatting. You do an amazing job.

Being an author is a solitary job by nature. Sometimes it can get lonely and overwhelming, so I'm grateful to the author friends I can turn to when the going gets tough: Jaimee Parker, Anna del Mar, Kali Anthony, Elle Thorpe, Miranda P. Charles, and Ruby Dixon. Thank you for your wisdom, understanding, and for making me laugh.

Thank you to my sister, Aimee, and my dear friends Diana, Melissa, and Jen for their constant support and encouragement.

But the biggest thank you of all goes to you, the reader. Thank you for reading my books and continuing to support me. Your kind words mean more than you could ever possibly know.

Manufactured by Amazon.com.au
Sydney, New South Wales, Australia

14853976R00079